THE LADY GRACE
MYSTERIES

Also available in

THE LADY GRACE MYSTERIES series

*

THE LADY GRACE MYSTERIES

MYSTERIES

GOLD!

Grace Cavendish

Jan Burchett and Sara Vogler are writing as Grace Cavendish

RED FOX

THE LA... ...RTEES GOLD
A RED FO... ...OOK 978 1 862 307...

... an ...imprint of... ...published in Great Britain by Doubleday,
...imprint of...ndom House Child...
...s Random House Group Company

Doubleday edition published 20...
Red Fox edition published 2006

7 9 10 8

Series created by Working Partners Ltd
Copyright © Working Partners Ltd, 2006

The right of Working Partners Ltd to be identified as the author of this work
has been asserted in accordance with the Copyright, Designs and Patents Act 1988.

**Penguin Random House is committed to a sustainable future for
our business, our readers and our planet. This book is made from
Forest Stewardship Council® certified paper.**

Printed and bound in Great Britain by Clays Ltd, St Ives plc

Set in Bembo

Red Fox Books are published by Random House Children's Publishers UK
61–63 Uxbridge Road, London W5 5SA

www.randomhousechildrens.co.uk
www.randomhouse.co.uk

Addresses for companies within The Random House Group Limited can be found at:
www.randomhouse.co.uk/offices.htm

THE RANDOM HOUSE GROUP Limited Reg. No. 954009

A CIP catalogue record for this book is available from the British Library.

To Lady Eloise Delamere,
ever your humble servants,
Jan and Sara

Most Privy and Secrete

The daybooke of my Lady Grace
Cavendish, Maid of Honour to
Her Gracious Majesty
Queen Elizabeth I of that name

At Her Majesty's castle, Windsor,
England

All Miscreants and Ill-wishers,
Keep Out

The Twentieth Day of April, in the Year of Our Lord 1570

In the Chapel of St George

It is five of the clock and I have escaped the hubbub in my chamber and found somewhere quiet to write in my new daybooke. I cannot abide any more of Lady Sarah Bartelmy as she dresses for supper. Sometimes it is very hard for Mary Shelton and me to share a bedchamber with Lady Sarah – she seems to fill the whole room.

There I was, sitting on my bed completely ready, my daybooke on my lap and a quill full of ink, when I was hit on the head by a ruff! Then two stomachers flew past my ear. In truth it was getting quite perilous. It seems that my fine Lady Sarah did not think they went well enough with her bodice. I fled, leaving her tiring woman, Olwen, to avoid the flying garments.

Now I have crept up the spiral staircase to the oriel window in St George's Chapel. I should be able to write in peace here. I love sitting in the oriel window. It looks out onto the altar and choir stalls, which are the special seats of the Knights of the Garter. Each seat is decorated with the knight's symbol and some are quite spectacular. My favourite banner is the one with the bright gold lion rampant on a black cloth – I do not know whose it is, but I like it because the lion looks very bold. At the moment there are some choristers chanting the daily prayer. They have no idea that I am here so I must stay quiet as a mouse!

Penelope Knollys, one of the other Maids of Honour, is soon to be wed in this very chapel. Penelope left Court a month ago to begin preparations, and before she went she gave me this daybooke as a keepsake.

'I could think of nothing more fitting, dear Grace,' she said. 'And I wager this will keep you out of mischief for a while!'

So I vow to use this daybooke as a record of her wedding and afterwards I may send it to her, for she is sure to be bored away from Court, and in need of some entertainment.

We have all known about Penelope's match with Thomas, her cousin, for some time, and of course the Queen was the first to be told. But a few weeks ago, when there was talk of setting the day, Her Majesty displayed her famous temper. She hates to lose any of her Maids of Honour.

We were all gathered in the Presence Chamber, and Penelope and Thomas approached Her Majesty to have a quiet word about the date when they should marry. At least they thought it would be a quiet word! Her Majesty let out such a roar that her guards were at her side in an instant.

'Are you hurt, My Liege?' asked one.

'I am stabbed to my very heart!' gasped the Queen, slumping in her chair. There was no sign of any blood, but I noticed that Penelope had gone as pale as her chemise. The guards looked at each other, not knowing quite what to do, for despite her words the Queen was obviously hale and hearty.

'You ungrateful Maid!' she bellowed at poor Penelope. 'How can you wish to leave my side and be wed?'

I could hardly keep from laughing! It was such a funny scene! At last the Queen was soothed by her Ladies-in-Waiting. She gave Penelope and Thomas her permission for the wedding to take place just three days from now, on St George's Day in St George's Chapel – how fitting!

'And, my dear,' the Queen told Penelope, as if the upcoming wedding was the best news she had ever had, 'this will be the most lavish wedding. I would have nothing less for one of my Maids!'

Her Majesty does blow hot and cold. She has nothing against Thomas, but in truth she does not wish to lose any of her Maids to marriage. In her heart she knows that we must all be married at some time, and indeed she tried to arrange a husband for me last year. But that was only because she is my godmother and wished to do her duty by me as I have no parents.

At least I shall not be displeasing her for a good long while. I cannot bear the thought of all that silly love nonsense and then being beholden to a husband. And anyhow, I have an important role at Court. It is most secret. People look at me and see only the Queen's youngest Maid of Honour. They do not know that I am also Her Majesty's Lady Pursuivant. Wrongdoers and enemies of the Queen beware: Lady Grace Cavendish will find you out!

Oh dear! Now I cannot send this daybooke to Penelope, for she will learn my secret! Mayhap I shall just read parts out to her when I see her.

But more of Penelope. Although I may not want romance for myself, I cannot help but be excited by this wedding. All the Maids of Honour have been in a fluster over it for weeks. Her Majesty completely forgot her initial heartbreak and ordered new gowns for us all. She can be most generous at times – and she always wants her Court to look splendid.

'I cannot have my Maids of Honour dressed

in last year's fashion!' she declared when we all tried to thank her.

After a day or two I began to wish she hadn't been so generous, for each time I stirred from my chamber someone jumped out at me with yards of silk and a handful of pins. But I have now got the most beautiful gown for my pains. It is of the finest yellow French silk; Mrs Champernowne, the Mistress of the Maids, says that it is most lucky for the bridesmaids to wear yellow, and she knows all the superstitions there are! The gown has slashed sleeves and delicate lace roses sewn with seed pearls. The lace is the Queen's own, a gift to her from the Venetian Ambassador. The front of the skirt is also slashed and I have a pale primrose forepart to wear beneath.

We do not know much about what Penelope's gown will be like. She has been at home with her mother and her sisters and all her cousins for the past month and has surely been putting up with even more pins than I have!

The bride and her family arrive tomorrow

and the Queen has ordered many festivities. On the day before the wedding we are to go on a hunt in the Great Park. This does not fill me with glee. I am no horsewoman and do not enjoy seeing the kill, but I will have to ride out nonetheless. Then there will be dancing in the evening. This does not fill me with glee either, but I would rather dance than ride. After the wedding ceremony itself there will be a feast and a performance by Mr Somers and his troupe of tumblers, which I always enjoy.

The following day Penelope and Thomas will leave for his estates in Staffordshire and everything at Court will return to normal. I will miss Penelope, for she is a good companion. I suppose she will have children and stay in the country and grow fat! The Queen does not have children at her Court, except for me when I was younger. My mother was her Lady-in-Waiting and closest friend, and Her Majesty did not wish to be parted from her even after I was born. Yet parted they were, in the end, by death. My mother died two years ago, when I was just twelve. She drank poisoned wine meant for the Queen, thereby saving Her Majesty's life. As my father had also died, I was left without parents, so the Queen made me her youngest Maid of Honour. I miss my mother dreadfully but the Queen ensures I want for nothing. Although she cannot show it, I know she cares for me deeply. She is my favourite person in the whole world.

The Court is full of people, which is nothing new, but for the last few days wedding guests have been arriving in droves. I am sure that some have come to give their good wishes to the couple, but plenty more are here because they want to be noticed by the Queen and given a position in her Household. As a consequence, there are many handsome young men around, and the Maids of Honour and Ladies-in-Waiting are in an absolute twitter. I think I am the only one who does not suffer from this particular disease, which makes the eyelashes flutter and the cheeks go pink. In Lady Sarah's case it also makes the bosom heave – and she has a lot of bosom to heave!

Of course Penelope is free from all this now

that she has caught Thomas. He is the second son of Sir Philip Penn, and although he has no inheritance, he has done well for himself in foreign trade. He is a minor twig in the great family tree of the Howards. (I am pleased with that phrase. Perhaps I shall use it in front of Her Majesty. She is fond of metaphors.) Penelope must become Penelope Penn – such a silly name – and she has to endure the most awful poetry from Thomas. However, Thomas is a good match, and handsome in his way. He has fair hair, and blue eyes that see no other maid but Penelope. So I think they suit each other well.

It is almost time for supper. Surely Lady Sarah must have finished dressing by now. I shall return my daybooke to my chamber and find out.

In my bed – very late

I think it must be nearly midnight. The Court is still at cards, but I could no longer hide my yawns and Her Majesty gave me leave to retire. She let Mary Shelton come with me, so I must make do with the light of just one candle, as Mary is trying to sleep. Lady Sarah is still playing cards and probably flirting with the gentlemen.

At supper the Queen was in a foul mood. All the extra people milling around had filled St George's Hall to bursting and I think they were a constant reminder that she is to lose one of her Maids to marriage!

I was sitting with the other Maids of Honour. Despite the number of people in the hall, the atmosphere was somewhat hushed. When Her Majesty is not in a good temper we all wish we could hide under the table. One poor servant nearly lost his head for daring to offer the Queen some wine. Well, in truth, she just shouted at him, but he looked as scared as if he were on the block already. I confess here in the privacy of my daybooke that I was glad not to be sitting too near her. Mr Secretary Cecil and my Lord Robert, the Earl of Leicester, were on either side and certainly had their work cut out trying to pacify her. The rest of us kept our speech to murmurs.

'It is lucky that Penelope is not here, for she would likely bear the brunt of Her Majesty's ill temper,' Mary Shelton whispered. 'What a pity that our Queen hates it when her Maids of Honour marry.'

'It is said that she has vowed to have no other husband than England, and expects the same loyalty from us,' Lady Jane Coningsby replied. Then she smiled. 'But that is a promise I fear I cannot keep and I hope that the same happiness comes to you all.'

Although I think this wooing is rather silly, I cannot but be pleased at the change it has wrought in Lady Jane. She is usually quite sour and, whatever I do, I seem to vex her. But she is much changed since Mr Naunton began courting her. She has even been quite pleasant to me! Yesterday I was late for prayers because I had been playing with Mr Will Somers's new puppies. They are so sweet and he hopes to train them to perform for Her Majesty in his tumbling troupe. Anyway, I was dashing round a corner when I crashed right into Lady Jane. I waited to be called a 'clumsy ragamuffin' or a 'foolish jackanapes', but she just smiled and asked me where I had been. I found myself telling her all about little Castor and Pollux and how they had licked my face and nibbled my fingers. She said they sounded sweet and she looked forward to seeing them with Mr Somers's troupe. It is most unlike her.

'I think the Queen is so against marriage because she cannot wed Lord Robert,' sighed Carmina Willoughby. We looked across to where Lord Robert, the Earl of Leicester, was trying to raise Her Majesty's spirits. Even he was not succeeding. 'If I were her I would marry him and ignore the gossips who whisper that his wife's death was no accident!' Carmina continued. She leaned forwards to be sure that only we could hear her. 'I wonder whether perhaps she is jealous of those who are free to wed.'

'What nonsense!' I told her hotly. I am becoming heartily sick of all these silly rumours and suppositions about our noble Queen. The absolute worst and most stupid is that she is fearful that Penelope will outshine her at the wedding. By my troth, no one could do such a thing, for whenever the Queen enters a room everybody else looks dull by comparison.

'It is all just tittle-tattle,' I went on. 'Mayhap the real reason lies in her childhood. Her father, the old King Henry, hardly set a good example for marriage!'

'I think you are right, Grace,' said Mary Shelton. 'For he kept the priests very busy with his many weddings.'

At that moment there was a loud oath from the Queen (which I will not write here for fear of setting my book alight!) and we all jumped in our seats. Lady Ann Courtenay had dripped a tiny bit of mutton grease onto Her Majesty's wrist ruff while serving her!

'This sheep must be accursed,' she complained, 'to torment me in this way! If it were not dead already, I would have it put to death!'

No one dared move. I paid close attention

to my salt fish fritters and I think my neigh-bours did the same.

'These are my favourite ruffs!' the Queen continued, unfastening them and throwing them to the floor. 'Now look at them, ruined beyond repair. Get them from my sight!' Poor Lady Ann looked as if she would faint as she picked up the ruffs and curtsied her way from the table.

At that moment a page timidly approached the Queen's chair, with deep bows all the way. He held out a sealed scroll to her.

'And what is this fresh torment?' growled the Queen, as she took the parchment, ripped the seal from the paper and unrolled it.

No sooner had she read the first few words than she lifted her head and beamed at us all. 'Ah, good news at last,' she said, waving the scroll at us. 'I am well pleased.'

Some of the guests were not used to Her Majesty's sudden changes of temper and they looked quite confused. I was itching to know what could have been in the letter to make Her Majesty so cheerful all of a sudden. I was not the only one. As soon as the page passed our table, Lady Sarah beckoned him over.

'Tell me,' she said with a pretty shake of her copper locks. 'What tidings did you bring the Queen? You have done us all a great service: you alone have brought the smile back to her face.'

The page leaned forwards, looking very pleased with himself. 'I cannot swear to the actual words, my lady,' he whispered, 'but I heard the messenger say that Her Majesty's loan was on its way at last and rests but fifteen miles from here.'

I wondered if the Queen would want us all to know this, but now that Lady Sarah had the news it would be around the Court before the end of the feast.

'Then her patience has been rewarded,' said Lady Sarah, waving him off with a gracious hand.

Patience! The Queen nearly had the roof off a week since, when she heard that the ship from Flanders carrying her loan had been delayed. It seems strange to me that though Her Majesty is so magnificent and has such glorious gowns and jewellery, she is always in need of ready cash – or gold and jewels, which are as good. Mrs Champernowne says that Her Majesty's wealth is all tied up in land and palaces and so she needs must negotiate with the Flemish bankers for a loan of gold and jewels. Certainly being Queen is a most complicated matter!

'No wonder the Queen is relieved,' said Mary Shelton. 'Her gold and jewels should have been safely in the Tower in London these past six days.'

'Then why are they coming here to Windsor?' asked Carmina. Carmina has only just come back to Court from her parents' home. It seemed she had not caught up with the news.

'If the ship had docked at Dover as it should have done,' Mary told her, 'the loan would have been taken straight to the Tower. But the vessel was blown off course and had to dock at Portsmouth.'

'So it is quicker to bring the gold and jewels here to Windsor,' I added. 'And it is a happy chance for us that the messenger arrived when he did, for I believe he saved us all from a royal thunderstorm.'

Indeed it was as if the sun had come out in St George's Hall. The Queen smiled upon us and everyone began to laugh and chatter. Well, everyone except Lady Sarah. Lady Sarah Bartelmy can be an amusing companion – when she is not throwing clothes – but as Her Majesty cheered up, she seemed to become ever more glum.

'What is the matter with Lady Sarah?' Carmina whispered in my ear. Sarah was sitting next to us, opposite Lady Jane, and was watching her, as she talked merrily of Mr Naunton's latest flattery, with an expression like a stuffed trout.

'She is sulking because Lady Jane has a better suitor than she,' I told Carmina quietly. 'And you know how those two fine ladies hate to be bested by each other.'

'Surely, Carmina, you have seen Mr Naunton showering Lady Jane with poems and songs?' enquired Mary Shelton.

Carmina nodded. 'But does not Lady Sarah have Sir Roger Spratling in tow?' she asked, puzzled. 'He is rich, and certainly a better catch than Mr Anthony Naunton.'

'It is well known that Sir Roger is mean with his money,' I laughed, forgetting to keep my voice down. 'That is why he stays so rich!'

Unfortunately Lady Sarah heard. 'Fie on you, Grace!' she exclaimed angrily. 'He would be showering me with precious jewels if Mr Naunton did not owe him so much money.' She cast a look upon Lady Jane that would have melted iron!

But Lady Jane did not rise to the bait – she is certainly much changed, and long may it continue. 'Oh, Sarah!' she sighed dreamily. 'Would that you were content with a song from your lover's lips, as I am.'

A song would not do Lady Sarah much good, I thought, for Sir Roger cannot sing a note!

Lady Sarah looked thoroughly vexed at that, so Mary Shelton quickly put her hand across the table and squeezed Sarah's.

'I am sure that when the money is repaid, Sir Roger will buy you the finest of presents,' she declared firmly.

Lady Sarah seemed soothed, but I could not resist winking at Mary, who nearly choked on her fish.

'Indeed,' Lady Sarah said, smiling at us all, 'he had better give me a fine present to show how eager a suitor he is, or I may find another to come wooing!' And with that, she looked around the room to see if any of the young men were looking her way.

A little later

I had to stop writing just now. Mary begged me to move my candle as the flickering was keeping her awake. So I have moved my candle to the other side of the bed, where it now teeters on a narrow window ledge and I can hardly see to write!

Before I forget I must scribble down an

amusing incident that happened at supper. A little while after the page had told us the news of the Queen's loan, one of the guests suddenly jumped to his feet. Everyone in St George's Hall went quiet and stared at him. He looked in terror at the Queen, muttered, 'Sick!' and quickly clapped his hand over his mouth! Then he clambered desperately over the bench he had been sitting on and rushed out backwards, trying to bow as he went. All the time his face was going greener and greener. As soon as he had gone a huge roar of laughter broke out, and Her Majesty laughed loudest of all.

'You had better look to your laurels, Mr Somers,' she told the master of her tumbling troupe, 'for Stephen Morling has given us great entertainment.'

Usually a courtier will not stay away from the Queen and her Court if he can possibly help it, for one cannot win the Queen's favour if one is not present. But poor Mr Morling did not return to the supper, or join us later for cards. I can only think he must have been very ill indeed!

The candle is guttering, but if I lean my daybooke sideways I can catch some moonlight from the window and see just well enough to write. Mary is sound asleep so I do not think I will disturb her.

After supper we moved into the parlour so that we could play cards. The servants brought along the little folding tables and arranged chairs around them. I sat with Mr Anthony Naunton, Lord Ruxbury and Lady Sarah to play Primero. Lord Ruxbury is to be Thomas's best man at the wedding. He is about the same age as Thomas – less than twenty, I think – and very handsome. This was not lost on Lady Sarah, who had little time to actually play cards, as she seemed determined to flirt with him – and she did not leave Mr Naunton out either.

She need not have given herself the trouble. Neither gentleman seemed to notice her efforts. Mr Naunton, of course, is entirely besotted with Lady Jane. And Lord Ruxbury was courteous to Lady Sarah but seemed blind to her charms! It was not as if he had another beauteous lady to talk to, for there was only me, though he chatted to me very pleasantly all the evening. For once I think Lady Sarah was jealous of me on account of it! Well, Lord Ruxbury is very tall and gallant with dark, twinkling eyes and a truly winning smile. I only write this to show why Lady Sarah was so displeased.

I told Lord Ruxbury all about the new puppies and in turn he related a lovely story about a kitten. It had made a home in one of his riding boots when he was a boy and he had had to make shift with an old pair that was far too small. It is so pleasant to talk with someone who seems to care for animals as I do. Usually I find it difficult to talk to the young gentlemen of the Court, but with Lord Ruxbury I felt quite at ease.

Mr Naunton dealt the second round and I found I was holding a chorus! A high one! I knew I could not be beaten with four sevens. When I declared my cards Lord Ruxbury seemed delighted and emptied the pot of winnings into my hands.

This was too much for my haughty Lady

Sarah. 'I am surprised you are so enjoying the cards, Grace,' she said sharply. 'You would not credit it, gentlemen, but she is usually scribbling in some silly daybooke or other.'

Lord Ruxbury looked at me.

'It is just something I write in now and again,' I muttered, blushing. 'I put down my thoughts . . . and meditations . . .'

'I wonder what those thoughts might be,' said Lord Ruxbury with a smile. 'I would love to know.'

I heard Lady Sarah give a disapproving sniff.

A few minutes later

Lady Sarah has just come to bed and made no effort to be quiet. She woke poor Mary Shelton and then turned on me, saying she could not sleep for my bright candle blazing!

''Tis nearer two of the clock than one, Grace,' she complained, 'and none but you and Mary were given leave to quit the cards early. Some of us are tired and need our rest!'

I cannot bear her nagging any more so I will cease writing.

The Twenty-first Day of April, in the Year of Our Lord 1570

Disaster has struck! It is eleven of the clock and I have escaped to the North Terrace, where I can write without being disturbed. It could be important to keep a record of the next few days. The Queen is beside herself with rage and even the wedding has been forgotten for the time being.

This morning I woke with a start to find Mrs Champernowne in our chamber. She was in a terrible flutter.

'What time is it?' I asked sleepily.

'Eight of the clock!' she clucked. 'Now get yourselves up, girls. Her Majesty needs you at once!' She poked her head out into the corridor. 'Olwen! Come dress your mistress without delay. Fran! Put those linens down, look you, and help with the other Maids!'

We staggered out of bed and pulled on our clothes as quickly as we could, with Olwen and

Fran fastening aiglets and sorting out petticoats. Lady Sarah started to moan that she had no time to attend to her hair but Mrs Champernowne silenced her with a frown.

'I wonder what can be the matter?' whispered Mary Shelton as we were ushered along to the Queen's Presence Chamber with Lady Jane and Carmina.

'Let us hope Her Majesty has not found another spot of grease,' I said.

As we neared the Presence Chamber there was a crowd of anxious courtiers pressing round the door. They parted on our approach. As we entered I could tell that this was nothing to do with grease on a ruff. The Queen would not have summoned the Gentlemen of the Guard to arrest a sheep. Yet five of the Guard were kneeling in front of her, and they were most pale. I wondered why they looked so scared. Next to them stood Mr Hatton, who is in charge of the Queen's Guard. Everyone in the room was silent – except the Queen.

'You dare to come into our presence,' she was bellowing at the trembling guards, 'and tell us that part of our loan has been stolen! How can this be?'

So this was the news that had stirred the Court so early. Theft of the Queen's property is grave indeed!

The guards cowered as if Her Majesty were breathing fire. I suppose I should not compare Her Gracious Majesty to a dragon, but she can certainly be as fierce!

'By God's light!' she thundered. 'Have your tongues been stolen as well?'

'My Liege,' said Mr Hatton solemnly, 'my men will answer, for they are loyal to Your Majesty and have nothing to hide. Here before Your Noble Presence are Henry Westerland and—'

'We know these men well!' snapped the Queen. 'Come, sirs, speak! We demand to hear the explanation of those who were charged with protecting our precious property!' She sank into her gilded chair and waited.

'Humbly begging Your Majesty's most gracious p-pardon . . .' stammered one of the guards nervously.

'No flowery words, Henry Westerland,' said the Queen more gently. 'Simply tell your story.'

'Your Majesty,' gulped the poor man, 'last night our party put up at the Black Cat Inn in Meadowfold, just fifteen miles from here. The five caskets of gold and jewels were stowed in an upper room, and heavily guarded.' He gestured towards the man next to him. 'Samuel Twyer was with me, patrolling the walls of the inn, and the other three gentlemen were inside, two at the door of the room and one within—'

'And with so many, still you could not keep safe our treasured loan!' the Queen stated flatly. 'How do you account for these thieving miscreants outwitting you all?'

'Your Majesty,' croaked Henry Westerland, 'I can give you no account of it. We neither heard nor saw anyone pass us in the dark. It was only when there were cries for help from inside the inn that we knew anything was amiss.'

'We were most vigilant, Gracious Majesty,' added Samuel Twyer earnestly.

'Not vigilant enough, it would seem,' murmured the Queen. 'And what of those who were stationed at the chamber door?'

Two of the kneeling guards bowed their heads in shame. Then one of them spoke. I could see he had a bloodstained bandage around his head.

'Most Gracious Queen,' he began in a terrified squeak, 'we were both knocked to the ground and knew no more until it was too late.'

'And I was within the chamber, Your Majesty,' added the guard at the end of the row. 'Suddenly a man burst in and—'

The Queen leaned forward, frowning in disbelief. 'One man?' she interrupted. 'You are telling us that this feat was accomplished by one man alone? We expected it to be a whole army of brigands at the very least!'

'There may have been more, Your Majesty, but there was only one man in the room with me,' whimpered the guard, wiping the sweat from his forehead. 'And he had a gun. He was very well-mannered and asked me most politely to help him stow the gold from one casket in his saddlebags. Though I had no choice, for he waved his gun at me.'

'And would you know this man again?' enquired the Queen coldly.

'No, My Liege, for his face was hidden by a black kerchief,' answered the guard. Then he brightened a little. 'But I would know the gun, for it was very fine and the villain had it pointed directly at my heart. The weapon had an ornate ivory handle and wheel-lock—'

'We are not concerned with the design of the gun, man!' the Queen snapped. 'We would have you tell us how this felon made clean away with our gold.'

'I tried to follow him,' explained the guard, 'but in vain, for he had barred the door and I could not push it open.'

'We came when we heard Hugh's calls, Your Majesty,' added Samuel Twyer quickly. 'We found him hammering on the door. The thief had lodged a broom handle through the candle sconces on either side of it.'

'And in the meantime,' remarked the Queen, 'the rogue had vanished.'

'He must have escaped through a window, Gracious Queen,' mumbled Henry Westerland, 'for we saw no sign of him.'

'I heard a whinny and the sound of horse's hooves from within my prison,' put in the guard called Hugh. 'I recall hearing the church clock striking the half hour – it would have been half after three,' he added helpfully.

The Queen looked as if she hardly knew why Hugh was telling her the time, but I committed it to memory, for it may be important later.

Mr Hatton stepped forwards quickly to get the story finished. 'Your Majesty,' he said, 'my men acted most swiftly. Twyer and Westerland took to their horses immediately. There is but one lane out of the village and they were soon in pursuit of the thief. They came to a crossroads and found a man sitting by the hedge. Although he was a little the worse for drink, his testimony was clear. He said that he had seen not one but three horsemen ride by only a minute ago, "as if the Devil himself and all his Hellhounds were after them".'

'But not our guards, it seems,' the Queen commented coldly.

'My Liege,' continued Mr Hatton steadily, 'the drunkard added that the villains did not have the look of skilled horsemen and were lucky to keep their seats. My men followed the direction that he gave, which took them deep into the forest, but they found no one. There was nothing to be gained by continuing to search in the dark so they returned to the inn. Here they were met by a shepherd who, knowing them to be the Queen's men, had a grievance to put before them. He told them that he had been bringing an orphaned lamb to his wife to be hand-reared, when he was nearly trampled by a horse and rider galloping from the inn in great haste. He said the horse must have been black, for he did not see it in the darkness until it was almost upon him. Perhaps the thieves had split up to escape our men.'

The Queen looked at the five guards and

sighed. 'Get you gone,' she said. 'And think yourselves fortunate we do not have you whipped for this bungling!'

The men scuttled out backwards, white in the face. But Her Majesty's Gentlemen of the Guard are well trained and loyal. The thieves must have been very clever to outwit them.

As soon as the guards had gone, the Queen turned to Mr Hatton. 'What is your opinion of this sorry affair, sir?' she demanded.

'I believe the thieves to be sturdy beggars!' answered Mr Hatton gravely. 'Ruffians through and through. They have likely disappeared into Windsor Forest. I will dispatch a band of my guard to search while there is daylight to aid them. I do not think the thieves will have journeyed far if they are such poor horsemen as our witness suggested.'

'Then do so and right swiftly,' ordered the Queen.

Mr Hatton swept a deep bow. 'I will leave no stone unturned until I find Your Majesty's missing gold and have the guilty parties in my grasp.'

The Queen dismissed him with a wave of her hand. Then she began to pace the room, her skirts rustling and her jewels rattling as she stomped about. I could see servants hovering round her, uncertain whether to approach with wine and sweetmeats.

Everyone started gossiping in undertones about the theft, but I stayed away from all the chatter. I wanted to think hard about what I had heard. Wrong had been done to Her Majesty. A fifth of her loan had been stolen! As her Lady Pursuivant, I wanted to start investigations without delay, but I knew the Queen would never allow me to venture into Windsor Forest in pursuit of thieves and ruffians. And as I thought about it, I realized that something about the story did not ring true to me.

Mr Hatton believed the thieves to be 'sturdy beggars', but it would surely be most unusual for some brigand from the forest to have such a valuable pistol as the guard had described. Of course, it was possible that it had been stolen in some other robbery, and yet we had also heard that the man in the room from which the gold was taken had been polite and well-mannered. It seemed strange behaviour for a ruffian, and I could not entirely share Mr Hatton's conclusion that this theft was the work of 'sturdy beggars'.

Suddenly it struck me that one or more of the thieves might be a courtier! It would explain the elaborate pistol and the gentle-manly behaviour. Of course, they could have fled with their booty and now be long gone, but anyone's sudden disappearance from Court in the current circumstances would immediately draw suspicion. I reasoned that if any courtiers had been involved in the theft, they would surely have returned to Windsor afterwards so that their absence would not be noted. And I realized that while I cannot scour the woods for sturdy beggars, I can investigate discreetly at Court to find out whether this theft might indeed have been carried out by a courtier. Surely that is a fitting job for Her Majesty's secret Lady Pursuivant, especially since Mr Hatton is focusing all his suspicions upon brigands in the forest. If only there were not so many newcomers at Court at present for Penelope's wedding! It would take a year to investigate them all. No matter, I will do my best. But first I must seek the Queen's permission.

I looked across to the Queen, who had stopped storming about like a tempest and had returned to her chair. She was alone and taking moody sips from a goblet of wine. I prayed that she was now calm enough not to throw the goblet at me.

I approached her and made a deep curtsy.

The Queen leaned forwards and grasped my arm. 'Grace,' she whispered, and I saw a flicker of anxiety in her eyes, 'I warrant you are about to offer me the services of my Lady Pursuivant. Yet I fear that this time there is nothing you can do. The brigands are far away.'

'Your Majesty,' I said softly, 'I am troubled by the account that the guards have given. I believe they speak the truth, but I cannot think that the thief they saw was a mere brigand. There smacks too much of the gentleman in his behaviour.'

I explained my suspicions to the Queen.

She listened intently and was silent for a moment when I had finished.

'You are my secret eyes and ears as always, dearest Grace,' she said finally. 'You may investigate here at Court. But not beyond its bounds. I would not have my dear god-daughter chasing brigands all around the Forest of Windsor.'

'As Your Majesty wishes,' I said obediently. But as I withdrew from her presence I suddenly had an image of the Queen's own Lady Pursuivant creeping about among the trees in the dark of the night, swathed in a long cloak and tracking bands of miscreants. I felt a pang of disappointment that I was to be confined to Court!

The Queen beckoned to Mr Hatton. 'Come,' she said to him. 'We will have more speech in my Privy Chamber. And, as the thieves were kind enough to leave me some of my loan, we must arrange for it to be safely housed here at Windsor.'

I realize that I am cold! It is a sunny day and the light is sparkling off the Thames below, but I am hidden in the shade and have no cloak. I shall put my book away and find a roaring fire before I start my investigations.

On the slope below the Round Tower

It is close to three of the clock. I am now sitting on the sunny grass and feeling much warmer. Lady Sarah would tell me that the sun is bad and will give me freckles. She has a horror of freckles, but with her red hair I suppose she is more disposed to them. I cannot resist the sun's warmth.

I have perched myself here because there is a wonderful view to the west. Penelope and her family will be arriving on the road from Newbury within the hour and I have resolved to be the first to see them! I am still determined to chronicle all the events of Penelope's wedding, even though I can now only read parts of my daybooke to her and cannot let her see inside for herself.

There is only a farm cart coming along the road at the moment and I do not think Penelope and her whole family could fit on that! I hope I shall have time to finish recording what I have discovered about the theft before they arrive.

After the Queen had departed the Presence Chamber with Mr Hatton, I considered where to begin my investigation. I thought I would first review what I knew of the theft.

The Black Cat Inn in Meadowfold is full fifteen miles from Windsor. It would take both excellent horsemanship and a swift mount to ride there and back in the space of one night, particularly as most of the courtiers were playing cards until nearly two in the morning. And anyone involved in the theft would have to make sure they were back at Court by first light, if they wanted their absence to go unnoticed.

From the guards' account, I could be sure there was at least one thief and possibly three, though all or none of them might have come from Court. I confess that that elegant ivory-handled pistol has given me a strange feeling that a gentleman courtier is behind this. We shall see if I am right!

I decided to begin my investigation by trying to find out whether any of the gentlemen who were at Court last night had behaved strangely. I am very proud of my tactics. They were simple. I would listen to the tittle-tattle! And where better to hear rumours and hearsay than among the Maids of Honour.

I made sure I sat between Lady Jane and Lady Sarah at dinner today. They are supreme experts in gossip. But I was to be sorely disappointed.

They were bickering about which of their suitors is the better. Well, Lady Sarah was trying to bicker. Lady Jane was just sighing over her sweetbreads.

'Mr Naunton may not have riches but he has a rich soul,' she said dreamily. 'His poetry is like music to my ears.'

'Fie on his poetry,' retorted Lady Sarah. 'That will not get you a new gown.'

'What do I care for new gowns?' Lady Jane said serenely.

I nearly choked on my mead at that!

'You have changed your tune since last week, Jane!' huffed Lady Sarah, drumming her fingers irritably on the table.

I gave up on them. Opposite me was Sir Arthur Fairbrother. I got no joy from him either, as he is rather old and was too interested in dunking his manchet bread in his wine and sucking on it noisily to pay me much attention. Poor man! He has hardly a tooth left in his mouth and so has to eat like a baby.

After the meal I joined Mary Shelton, Carmina and some of the Ladies-in-Waiting in St George's Hall, hoping I would have more luck. They were decorating the huge chamber with beautiful hangings, gaily coloured ribbons and silk cushions in readiness for the coming revels. Mary had gathered ivy and herbs to make garlands and the hall smelled lovely.

Carmina and Lady Margaret Symonds were winding pale blue silk around a column. Tomorrow they will be weaving freshly picked forget-me-nots into it.

Lady Margaret greeted me with a smile. 'Perhaps you can cast light on something for me, Grace dear,' she said. 'I have been asking Carmina about the colour of Penelope's wedding gown and she does not know any details.'

'I have heard it is red,' I said quickly, as Penelope told me before she left Court that she wanted to be married in red.

'And are the sleeves of cobweb lawn?' Lady Margaret asked. 'And is it true she has a ruff in the new French style?'

I had to admit that I did not know, as all the arrangements for Penelope's dress have been made at her home and we have not been privy to them. I tried to bring the subject round to the newcomers at Court, but Lady Margaret wanted only to talk of dressmaking.

As soon as I could, I made the excuse that Mary Shelton needed my help and slipped away. Mary was directing a servant who was balanced precariously on a ladder. He was hanging some garlands of rosemary and ribbons around a tapestry and Mary was deciding where the leaves would drape at their best.

I must have looked preoccupied as I approached, for Mary took my hand.

'Are you not enjoying all this excitement, dear Grace?' she said. She felt my forehead. 'You are not sickening for anything, are you? I do hope you have not been eating the same food as poor Mr Morling last night!'

I think that at the same instant we both remembered the poor man's hasty exit from the hall and we burst out laughing. Mary was very naughty, for she did a wonderful impersonation of Mr Morling, looking cross-eyed and sick. And it was then that something came to me. Mr Morling had left the supper table early last night and had not returned for the rest of the evening. We had all thought him ill, but what if he had been dissembling and had instead ridden to Meadowfold and the Black Cat Inn? Lady Sarah had said that everyone but Mary Shelton and me had been playing cards until well after one of the clock. So Mr Morling, who was too sick to play, had had more time than any of the other courtiers to ride to Meadowfold. I felt he definitely merited further investigation.

'Do you know anything of Mr Stephen Morling?' I asked Mary, trying to look as if I wasn't much interested.

'Very little,' she replied. 'He is newly arrived at Court. Aside from showing himself to have a weak stomach, I did hear that he is a very poor horseman.'

My ears pricked up at that. Had not Mr Hatton's men been told that the thieves could barely keep their seats?

'How do you know?' I asked. I had to be sure.

'Mildred told me,' she explained. 'You know Mildred. She works in the Great Kitchen and furnishes me with rose-water for my face. She is sweet on Perkin in the stables and he told her that it was a miracle Mr Morling stays in the saddle when he rides!'

Mary knows everyone! If she was so inclined she would make a good Lady Pursuivant, but she does not have the temperament. She is too kind and will not like to suspect anyone. I have no such worries. And now it looks as if I have a real suspect!

There was an embarrassed cough from above. We both looked up to see the poor servant practically hanging from the tapestry. I left Mary to rescue him and returned to Lady Margaret and Carmina, determined to make them tell me what they knew of Mr Stephen Morling.

Lady Margaret and Carmina had not got much further with their silk. They seemed to be discussing every wedding they had ever known and it was difficult to get a word in!

'I was wondering,' I said quickly, as Carmina took a breath, 'whether any wedding has ever attracted so many visitors. There is a whole bevy of people I have never set eyes upon and know nothing of! For example, who is Mr Stephen Morling?'

'Now, I wonder why you want to know about Stephen Morling, Grace,' Carmina giggled. 'Are you smitten perchance? Should we be expecting another wedding soon?'

Before I could reply, Lady Margaret took my arm. 'I would not think of him as a suitor, Grace,' she said seriously. 'It seems he is a spendthrift who has used up all his money and is now seeking a position at Court. I expect he hopes to become a Gentlemen Guard like his brother, Hugh.'

So Mr Morling is in need of funds! I found that most interesting. It gives him reason to have carried out the theft.

I needed to see my friends Ellie and Masou. Ellie often hears tittle-tattle from the servants as she goes about her work in the laundry. I thought she might be able to find out whether Stephen Morling had indeed been lying sick in his bed last night. And Masou and his fellow members of Mr Somers's troupe are always milling around the castle. One of them may even have seen Mr Morling leave. I was about to seek them out when Mrs Champernowne caught me.

'Where do you think you're going, Grace, my girl?' she enquired. 'Do you not remember that we have the cover for Penelope's marriage bed to finish?'

This would not help me find my friends. The other Ladies and Maids were gathering to work on the beautiful cover Mrs Champernowne had brought in. We are embroidering the edges with primroses and Lent lilies. It is very delicate work and needs much patience. I sat down, knowing we would be there for hours. I soon realized there was only one thing I could do. I had to make a supreme sacrifice in the service of Her Majesty. I decided I must prick my finger.

I would not have credited before how hard it is to prick a finger. I do it all the time by accident. But to do it on purpose proved almost impossible. There was my finger; there was the needle. It should have been so simple to stab myself with it. In the end I had to close my eyes and hope I hit my mark. I did! And it hurt so much that I nearly let out an oath. But it worked. Mrs Champernowne took one look at the tiny droplet of blood and banished me from the quilt without further ado.

'Thomas and Penelope will not thank you

for adding your own colour, look you, Grace,'
she snapped. 'Go and staunch that wound.'

A few moments later

My attention was caught just now by some
movement out to the west. I put down my
daybooke and jumped up, ready to greet the
wedding party. But it turned out to be a herd
of deer dashing across the road and making for
the trees.

Anyway, I hurried from St George's Hall
before Mrs Champernowne could change her
mind. Now I was free to find Ellie and Masou.
Sucking my finger – which still hurt – I went
down to the laundry rooms. With luck I would
meet only kind Mrs Twiste, wife of the Master
Launderer, who would not question why I
needed Ellie.

Ellie was pounding cuckoo-pint roots to
make starch and I could see her hands looked
even more sore than usual. Ellie hates that job.

'Them roots sting me skin something cruel,' she says.

I had just beckoned to her to come with me when a familiar voice grated in my ear.

'Can I help you, my lady?' It was the dreaded Mrs Fadget, the Deputy Laundress, who always wants to be the one to assist a Maid of Honour.

'You are most kind, Mrs Fadget,' I said quickly, 'but it is merely a matter of a tiny spot of blood on a kerchief – far too trivial for someone as important as you to trouble with. I would not take you from your starching, for no one can set a ruff as you do.'

The miserable old laundress began to simper. 'Indeed, Lady Grace,' she said, 'I learned my craft from none other than Mistress van der Passe.'

She seemed to think I should be impressed, but I just took Ellie by the arm. 'Come. You will do,' I said imperiously as I marched her to the door.

As soon as we had got out into the Kitchen Court we collapsed in giggles.

'Did you see her face?' gasped Ellie. 'She

looked like a fox that had had the chicken snatched from it!'

'She usually looks more like a chicken!' I snorted and we collapsed again. 'Who is Mistress van der Passe anyway?' I asked.

'Mrs Fadget always goes on about her,' sighed Ellie, pushing her tangled hair from her eyes. 'She's a Flemish woman who Mrs Fadget says is the last word in starching. I don't think she's even met her!'

'What is going on here?' came a stern voice.

We whipped round, thinking we had been caught out. But it was only Masou, grinning all over his face.

'Why should a Maid of Honour and a laundrymaid lurk by the rubbish tip?' he asked, his dark eyes full of mischief. 'I do hope it is the tip that smells so foul and not my dear ladies!' He held his nose dramatically and fell back as if overcome by the stench, turning his fall into a clever backward roll. Masou often boasts that he is the best of Mr Somers's tumblers. Indeed, he says he was the best in all Africa, though he left there when he was very little!

Ellie picked up a rotting carrot top and threw it at him. 'We couldn't smell anything till you arrived, Masou,' she laughed.

Then we heard a door open and quickly ducked down out of sight. It makes me very sad that I have to keep my friendship with Ellie and Masou secret. It is not thought seemly for a Maid of Honour to have such lowly friends. As for me, I could not wish for two more loyal companions. The Queen is the only person who knows about our friendship – though she has to pretend she has no such knowledge or she would have to forbid my seeing them.

A splattering of apple peelings was thrown onto the tip. I waited until the footsteps had died away, and then picked an apple core out of my hat.

'I must speak with you both urgently,' I whispered to my friends. 'Let us find somewhere less dangerous.'

'What about the Horseshoe Cloister?' Ellie suggested. 'There's nothing but clerics there and they'll have their noses stuck in their prayer books. No one will notice us.'

'Well spoken, fair Ellie,' said Masou. 'Yet we must make our journeys there by diverse routes, for it would not do for us to be seen with such a dolt as Grace!'

I tried to pinch him, but as usual he was too nimble and darted out of the way.

'We shall see your ladyship by the lodgings of the illustrious clerics,' he said, and vanished.

When Masou and Ellie were gone I set off across the Tilting Yard, through the Inner Gatehouse and down the slope past St George's Chapel to the cloister beyond. I did not see Ellie and Masou on my journey, yet somehow they contrived to be there before me! Of course, a Maid of Honour should not be seen running, or I am sure I would have beaten them both.

Ellie and Masou were sitting on one of the low walls of the cloister, kicking their heels.

'What took you so long, Grace?' asked Ellie, trying not to pant. 'We have been here this last half hour!'

I ignored her teasing; I had more important things to talk about. 'I need your help with a most important matter,' I told them.

Masou waved his hands mysteriously in front of my nose. 'Let me divine what is in your thoughts,' he muttered, making ridiculous faces at me. 'By the power of the great pyramids of Al Jizah, the magic fingertips have it. Someone royal and close to us here has been robbed of something precious. You are about to seek our help in finding it, and bringing the malefactors to justice.'

'That is exactly it!' I said.

Ellie's eyes grew wide with fright. 'You read her mind, Masou! Don't you come near me with them magic fingertips.'

'Have no fear, Ellie,' I grinned. 'Masou is no more a soothsayer than I am. He must have heard the Court gossip; that is all!'

'You varmint, Masou!' cried Ellie, poking him in the ribs. 'I thought you'd been dabbling in the black arts! Anyway, what is the gossip? That old bat Fadget has had me head in the starching vat since sunrise. I've seen no one all morning aside from her. I've not even had any lunch.'

I felt very guilty. Ellie never gets enough to eat and my head had been so full of the robbery that I had given no thought to bringing her anything.

'Let me see what I can conjure up for you,' murmured Masou. 'Al Jizee, Al Jizah, Al Jizoo!' he chanted solemnly. Then he plunged his hand into his jerkin and produced a chunk of oatmeal bread. 'Ah, but Ellie,' he said with a mischievous twinkle in his eye, 'I have just realized that, of course, you will not wish to partake of this bedevilled food. No matter – I will eat it myself!'

'No you won't!' exclaimed Ellie, snatching the bread from him. Masou laughed as she tried to put it all into her mouth in one go.

'Come on then,' she demanded, spitting breadcrumbs. 'What's all this about losing something precious?'

'You truly have had your head in the starch all morning, for the whole Court is talking of Her Majesty's loan,' said Masou.

'Why?' asked Ellie. 'What has happened to it?'

'The gold and jewels from one of the five caskets has been stolen,' I told her.

Ellie nearly choked on the bread.

'By twenty brigands,' added Masou. 'Twenty brigands in full armour, with cannons and swords and—'

'Do not listen to him, Ellie!' I said. 'That is arrant nonsense!' I related the whole story. 'Now, I have one possible suspect,' I finished.

'Who's that then?' asked Ellie crossly. 'I warrant it's some foreigner. One of them Scots, I'll be bound. Mrs Fadget is always going on about them and their wild ways.'

'No, indeed,' I told them. 'I believe it is someone much nearer to hand. Do you know anything of Mr Stephen Morling?'

They both shook their heads.

'He could be one of the thieves,' I said. 'On the night of the robbery he left the supper table early and did not rejoin the rest of us that evening. That means he had plenty of time to meet any accomplices and ride to Meadowfold and back. Also, I have heard that he is always short of money. And his brother was one of the guards escorting the gold.'

'Do you suspect the brother as well, Grace?' asked Masou.

I thought about this for a moment. 'In truth, no,' I said at last. 'Mr Hatton chooses his Gentlemen of the Guard for their honesty and loyalty and I doubt he would have been able to hide his guilt in front of Her Majesty as he did this morning.'

'So how did the thief know where to go?' demanded Ellie. 'Sounds like witchcraft after all.'

'There was no magic involved,' I laughed. 'We all knew that the gold lay fifteen miles away along the Portsmouth road. It would not be hard to find out that the only village at that distance was Meadowfold.'

Ellie was fuming by now. 'How dare anyone do that to our Queen's rightful property!' she exclaimed, jumping from the wall and waving her fists. 'If I get hold of them thieves, I'll . . . I'll . . . boil 'em in me copper!'

'I would sooner face Her Majesty than Ellie and her copper!' laughed Masou. 'So, Grace, you think that Mr Morling is one of the felons involved?'

'Not necessarily,' I said. 'That is what we need to find out. Was he ill in his chamber or did he slip out? Can you ask among the servants?'

'Your wish is our command,' said Masou eagerly. He jumped down and swept a bow. 'Come, Ellie, we must waste no time. It is clear that the Queen's own Lady Pursuivant cannot do without us – as usual!'

By two-headed Janus! I can see the wedding party! They are already coming up Castle Hill. Some of the Gentlemen of the Guard are riding alongside. Mr Hatton must have dispatched them earlier when news of the robbery was heard, to give them safe escort. I can see Penelope on her white mare, Juno. Thomas gave her Juno as a betrothal gift and I will never forget the ecstatic look on her face when he presented the mare to her.

Penelope is wearing a fine velvet cloak and

a hat with peacock feathers. Her mother and father are riding with her, on either side of a most sumptuous litter carried by four strong-looking men. I cannot tell who is inside, for the curtains are drawn. Behind are more riders than I can count. Then there is a whole host of carts carrying clothes chests, boxes and servants. Other servants are walking behind the carts and the whole line stretches back into the village. I can see villagers at the roadside cheering and touching their caps. It is quite a sight. I am going to give them a wave!

No one saw me wave, though I nearly took off like a bird I was flapping my arms so wildly! I will run down to greet them.

Nine of the clock, in my bedchamber

Supper has just finished and I have managed to escape the company, but I dare not be long or Her Majesty will be displeased. I must make an entry in my daybooke now, for I cannot face Lady Sarah and Mary Shelton's moaning if I am scribbling away into the small hours again. And there is talk of playing cards once more this evening. I do not want to miss that.

Anyhow, back to this afternoon. As soon as I had closed my daybooke I slid down the slope, and ran through the Inner Gatehouse and into the Tilting Yard, remembering to slow down to a sedate walk as soon as I was out in the open. I was just in time! Penelope and her family were riding in through the King's Gate. The company filled the Tilting Yard! I have heard since that many cousins and friends have had to seek lodgings in the village.

The litter I'd seen was carrying Penelope's grandmother. I would not like to have been one of the bearers. Old Lady Knollys has a fearful temper that almost matches the Queen's. I think she would wish to punish every bump!

It was hard to get near to Penelope, but she saw me and we waved to each other. I tried to go forwards to greet her as she dismounted, but she was swallowed up and borne off as the party made its way inside.

Suddenly Carmina appeared and tucked her arm through mine. 'It is so exciting, Grace!' she squealed. 'Did you see that lovely riding habit Penelope was wearing? Her father paid for that. I hear he has been most generous.'

I knew why Penelope's father had been so generous. He had no choice! You cannot have a wedding at Court and be penny-pinching about it. The Queen would have something to say.

Carmina sighed. 'I hope my wedding will be as fine as this – whenever that may be.' She squeezed my arm mischievously. 'But I had forgotten – you will be the next bride, Grace! Once Mr Morling's stomach has recovered.'

I wished she would forget about Mr Morling – although *I* could not. I knew I had to make more enquiries but I would have to wait until supper.

St George's Hall was full to bursting at supper time. The guests who were lodged in the village had come to join the festivities. The Queen was at her most gracious and kindly let Penelope sit at her side. All attention was on them.

I happened to catch Lord Ruxbury's eye as I made for my seat. He swept me a most charming bow. I hope I shall see him later at cards – but only because he is such a good player and a pleasant companion. I then caught sight of Mr Morling. He was looking rather pale. (Of course, if he wanted to feign illness, he could achieve that by applying white lead to his face.) I tried to see if he ate much but it was hard to watch, for all the people in the way. (And I was not going to look too eagerly at him for fear that Carmina would notice and carry on with her daft comments!)

Mary Shelton and I were seated with some of the young men of the Court. This was luck indeed. Although they are fairly silly, at least I could ask questions about Mr Morling and not be accused of wishing to marry him!

'Stephen Morling, my lady?' said my neighbour, when I mentioned his name. 'Who is he, pray?'

'You know!' guffawed his friend next to him. 'The one who puked up his lobster last night.'

'Poor man,' I exclaimed in my most concerned tone. 'Was he very ill?'

'Well,' said the first, 'I didn't see him vomit, but I warrant that lobster had only one way to go!'

His companions roared with laughter. I gave up. I still did not know whether Mr Morling had really been ill last night or not. It was most vexing!

We soon left the supper table and made our way down to the Banqueting Hall in the Tilting Yard. We had a wonderful array of desserts, and even preserved medlars! Mr Will Somers's troupe was passing among the crowd, and I could see Masou, juggling and doing tricks as he went. He raised his eyebrows at me as he passed, and I knew he must have something to tell me so I followed him. Suddenly Mr Somers popped up in front of me. Without a word, he leaned forwards and produced an almond from my ear! I could not help laughing.

'You are a marvel, Mr Somers,' I told him, trying not to lose sight of Masou.

''Tis but a trifling piece of magic,' he replied. ''Twould take a good deal more skill than I possess to conjure up a flower for such a fair lady.' And, with that, he held out his hand and opened it to reveal a perfect little primrose. I gasped.

'Ah, Lady Grace,' he sighed comically, 'your beauty enhances my power!'

What a lot of nonsense he spouts, but his tricks are so clever! One day I will find out how he does them!

I threaded the stalk of the flower onto my bodice. 'Thank you, kind sir,' I said with a curtsy, as he left me and approached the Queen. I wondered what he would conjure up for her.

Thanks to Mr Somers I had lost Masou in the crowd. I thought he had become invisible until I heard a great burst of laughter. When I looked over, I caught sight of him surrounded by a circle of admiring courtiers. Masou is such a show-off! He had somehow cleared a space in the crush and was walking on his hands and juggling balls with his feet. Suddenly, with a kick, he sent them spiralling into the air to be caught by two giggling Ladies-in-Waiting. Then he did a handspring and landed upright.

'Masou!' I called. 'I promised the Count de Feete that you would perform some of your tricks for him. Come this instant. He awaits you outside.'

It is always hard for me to talk to Masou as a mistress to a servant. In truth, I had to fight to keep from laughing as he pulled all manner of faces to show me deference. He followed me out of the Banqueting Hall, bowing all the way, but I noticed that he still had time to snatch a handful of marchpane as he went.

When we got out into the Tilting Yard Masou looked around, puzzled. 'So where is this count, Grace?' he asked.

'There is no such person, you dunderhead!' I laughed. 'It was just an excuse to speak to you, away from everyone else. Count de Feete —

count–er–feit. See? It was just a play on words!'

'I am most disappointed,' said Masou mournfully. 'I hoped to gain favour with a foreign nobleman!'

I was beginning to feel sorry for having raised his hopes when Masou winked and grinned at me. I opened my mouth to chide him for tricking me, but he popped a piece of marchpane in it!

'You fiend!' I exclaimed, when I had finally stopped spluttering. 'You knew all along! Now I will brook no more of your silliness. Tell me what you have found out.'

'Your Mr Morling is nothing but a grey moth,' said Masou. 'He is dull and insubstantial and merely flits about the Court. I can find nothing of interest about him, except that lobster does not seem to agree with him. He looks an unlikely robber.'

'But it could be all pretence,' I insisted, unwilling to give up my only suspect so far. 'Somehow I must find out!'

'You could ask the Count de Feete!' Masou laughed and cartwheeled off.

And now I must put my daybooke under my pillow and return to the cards. I do not want anyone wondering where I am.

The Twenty-second Day of April, in the Year of Our Lord 1570

The clock in the watchtower has just struck eight. I have brought my daybooke down to the Tilting Yard and I am sitting in the sun again. Lady Sarah would have a fit!

I was woken early by the sunlight streaming through the windows. It was a perfect chance to go and see Ellie. I could ask her what she had found out about Mr Morling without too many listening ears. I was dressed in a trice in a simple chemise, bodice and kirtle. First I went to the Great Kitchen. We may have had a plentiful supper last night, but I was hungry now! And I did not want to meet Ellie empty-handed.

The Great Kitchen was full of the most wonderful smells of bread, herbs and roasting meat. It is an enormous place, bustling with servants, and it took me several minutes to find the Head Cook.

'As you see, Master Jenkins, I cannot sleep,' I told him. 'Can you spare me some bread, for I have woken with a gnawing hunger?'

'Anything for you, Lady Grace,' he beamed, as he cut a huge chunk from the manchet bread that was cooling from the oven. 'Pray seat yourself at the bench here.'

Soon I had a fine platter of bread and ham in front of me. I made sure to slip some up my sleeve for Ellie as soon as Master Jenkins went off to draw me some ale.

When he returned he was surprised to find my plate finished so quickly. 'It does me proud to see a good appetite,' he said happily, pushing a bowl of apples towards me. 'And what an honour for the kitchen to have noble company two mornings in a row. At this rate there'll be naught but scraps left for Her Gracious Majesty!'

'And I thought I was the only early riser,' I said, hoping he would tell me who had been there yesterday. If by chance it was Mr Morling, it would give me some idea of when he might have arrived back at Court after the robbery.

Perhaps missing most of supper and riding to Meadowfold and back again had given him an appetite!

'Lord Ruxbury was the earlier!' Mr Jenkins told me. 'It cannot have been much after five when he came in, for I was only just up myself and heard the tower clock strike the hour. Lord Ruxbury was still in his night garb, but he said he had such a hunger that I must needs fetch a physician or fill his belly quickly! You are like two peas in a pod!'

I suppose I am rather like Lord Ruxbury in other ways too. We are both fond of animals and we both have a brain in our heads – which is more than can be said for most of the young courtiers!

But I am straying from my purpose. I left the kitchen and went across the Horn Court to the laundry rooms in search of Ellie. She was stirring a pan of starch. I passed her the food I had brought. The bread disappeared quickly but she lingered over the ham, savouring it.

'I've been hoping you'd come, Grace,' she

said, when she had finished. 'I've got news for you!' She took me into the washing room and pointed at a large vat. It stank!

'That's Mr Morling's sheets in there,' Ellie told me, wrinkling her nose in disgust. 'I were that cross when his manservant brought them down late last night. They were covered in all sorts of spew and I tell you, old fish don't smell good. I can't see why they had to keep 'em all day 'cause the stains got really set in. Mrs Fadget said it were all my fault and I'd better see 'em white again or she'll know the reason why. I've had 'em soaking in ten-day-old urine through the night.'

'Are you sure they are from the night of the robbery?' I asked.

'I've washed more sick off linen than you've had hot suppers, Grace,' said Ellie proudly. 'And I'm sure. His servant said he'd been up all that night with 'is master, holding 'is head and fetching clean bowls and . . .'

I didn't listen to any more. I wished to keep the bread in my stomach! I will not be eating lobster for many a month!

So it seems that Mr Morling was truly ill, and I am left without a suspect. But the thief's polite behaviour, and his unusually fine pistol, still lead me to believe that he may have been a courtier, even if Mr Hatton does not think so.

All the castle will be waking up now. I must dress myself properly and join the other Maids for breakfast.

Evening, an hour before supper

I have a new suspect! And I think he is much more likely to be the thief than the last!

I am sitting in a stone alcove in the Larderie Passage. Although there is much bustle in the kitchens beyond, it is quiet here. This is the first time I have been able to write in my daybooke since this morning, for there has not been a minute to spare.

It was not long after breakfast when I came across a new clue. We were all in the Presence

Chamber attending Her Majesty while she signed some boring old letters that Mr Secretary Cecil kept thrusting under her nose. Well, he was not really thrusting them under her nose, he was passing them politely, but he looked very determined not to go until she had signed them all.

Lady Sarah had been having a private conversation with Sir Roger Spratling in a corner. She came over to us with a huge smile on her face. 'Look at this!' she whispered, holding out a silver necklace with a pendant of emeralds and pearls. 'Sir Roger has just given it to me!'

'It is indeed lovely,' said Mary Shelton, leaning forwards for a closer look.

'He rode all the way to London and back to buy it for me last night,' Lady Sarah sighed. 'You should have heard him, "My only goddess," he declared, "I have always longed to give you a gift to match your beauty. But as I cannot pluck the stars from the sky, I hope you will accept this humble trinket in their stead."'

When I was sure that Lady Sarah could not

see me, I struck a silly pose with my hands over my heart to make Mary laugh.

'So he has been generous at last!' said Carmina bluntly. 'We had thought him a skinflint— Ouch!' She broke off, for Mary had dug her in the ribs.

'He is no skinflint, Carmina,' said Lady Sarah. 'As you will recall, he was owed a large sum of money by Mr Naunton, who has now paid his debt in full.' I waited for her to add a barbed comment to Lady Jane about her unworthy suitor, but to my surprise she did not! (The necklace has certainly sweetened her temper!)

'Mr Naunton paid his debt as soon as he had the money,' said Lady Jane with a smile, 'for he is an honourable gentleman.'

My ears pricked up at this exchange. So Mr Naunton has suddenly acquired a large sum of money! And he seems to have acquired it since the robbery! I was eager to find out where it had come from. I was wondering how to ask without arousing suspicion, when Carmina came to my rescue.

'Where did he get the money?' she blurted out. I held my breath while I waited for the answer.

'That is not a question I would ask a gentleman,' said Lady Jane calmly. 'And I do not look to Mr Naunton for his wealth. Let me read you the poem he gave me this morning: "Jane, o Jane, I know not how, I do not kiss thy beauteous brow. The brow that gleams so pale i' the moon . . ."'

I could not listen to any more – and not only because it was nonsense. My mind was racing. I little wished to suspect the gentleman who has brought about such a delightful change in Lady Jane, but it looked as if Mr Naunton could be the thief!

I decided I would show a great interest in Mr Naunton and get Lady Jane to tell me all she knew about him. It is not usually difficult to get those in love to talk about their suitors. But at that moment the Queen signed her last paper with a flourish and rose.

'My duty is done!' she exclaimed. 'Let us prepare for the hunt!'

Fie on the hunt! It would seem that obstacles are thrown in my path at every turn!

So it was off to our bedchambers to get ready. Hunting was the last thing I wished to do. I had to find out about Mr Naunton and now I would have to do it from the saddle. It would to be hard to concentrate on being the Queen's Lady Pursuivant and ride at the same time. Why we have to charge around on horses just because someone is getting married, I know not!

It was a great surprise to me, but I actually enjoyed the hunt for once. I have a new hunting kirtle of gold velvet and a fine hat to match. Mrs Champernowne mutters and moans about me growing all the time, but what am I to do? And besides, it is pleasant to have new clothes.

The Court assembled in the Tilting Yard, where our horses were conveniently brought to us – although, because there were too many people for all to mount their horses in the Tilting Yard, those of lower birth had to walk down to the stables and meet their horses there.

The Queen was greeted by the Ranger of the Great Park, Sir Henry Neville, and a toast was drunk in mead warmed with a glowing poker. They rode out together through the King's Gate, and we all followed them the length of the Home Park and into the Great Park itself. I saw that the Earl of Leicester was close behind the Queen. I knew that the two of them would be setting the pace for the hunt and not many would keep up, which would not bother the Queen over much; she is most happy in the company of her 'Robin'.

Penelope and her sisters passed me by as I reached Langlands Walk. They are good horse-women and I was pleased that Penelope would enjoy the hunt held in her honour. I intended to ride sedately with the other Maids and not risk showing myself up in front of all the newcomers to Court. I noticed that Sir Roger Spratling stayed close to Lady Sarah, who was wearing his gift.

I steered Doucette in Lady Jane's direction. 'Where is your Mr Naunton?' I called to her.

'He will be here without delay, I am sure,'

replied Lady Jane, looking around anxiously. 'He is of the party that met their mounts at the stables.'

So, I thought, Mr Naunton is not from such an important family. That was all the more reason for him to be short of money. But that was the only cause I had to suspect him. It occurred to me that during the hunt I would get the chance to see whether he was a poor horseman. If he was, then that would tie in with the drunkard's description of the miscreants in Meadowfold.

However, even as that occurred to me, I remembered something else. One of the guards had mentioned that he heard a clock striking half past three as the thief galloped away. I knew that Mr Naunton had been playing cards until well after one. To have ridden the fifteen miles to Meadowfold by half after three, he would have to be an accomplished horseman indeed. It was a strange contradiction. Mayhap the drunkard was mistaken . . .

'I am pleased that Mr Naunton's fortunes have changed,' I said, 'for I have heard he is no longer in debt to Sir Roger Spratling. Mayhap you have brought him luck! Was it a gambling debt?'

'No indeed!' declared Lady Jane hotly. 'Mr Naunton is one of the few who avoids the lure of the cards!'

If he does, I am sure it is only to impress Lady Jane. Most gentlemen enjoy gambling. 'But I saw him at the card table two nights since,' I ventured. This could be important.

'He only played because it was the Queen's desire,' smiled Lady Jane, 'and would not have played otherwise. In truth, just after midnight he begged leave of the Queen to retire and write some more of his melodious poetry. Of course, he was too clever to mention that the verses were not for Her Majesty.'

So Mr Naunton had had time to ride to Meadowfold without being a gifted horseman! I had thought that no one but Mary Shelton and me had left St George's Hall early. Pretending to write verses for Her Majesty was a clever excuse. Before I could think any more on the matter Lord Ruxbury came into view. He galloped towards us on a most majestic black mare with white socks and a brilliant white blaze on her nose. She had a beautiful arched neck and her flanks gleamed in the sunlight. It looked as if the rider and his horse were one. As usual, I felt envious of someone who could ride so well. I was surprised that he had not ridden in the Queen's party, which was well out of sight ahead of us.

We were now progressing up the Greens Walk. Lord Ruxbury doffed his hat to us Maids and nodded his head towards Sir Roger Spratling. Then he appeared to lose his grip on the hat, which flipped up in the air behind him. In a flash he had his feet out of the stirrups and had turned to face his horse's tail. He caught his hat, tapped his mare with it and trotted round still facing backwards! It was so funny. It was as well that the Queen did not see him. She demands that the gentlemen of the Court have eyes for her alone and does not approve of anyone horsing around for the benefit of her Maids! (There – I have made a pun that Mr Will Somers himself would be proud of.)

Lord Ruxbury spun round again in the saddle, took up the reins and came to ride beside me.

'You have a fine mount, Lord Ruxbury,' I said. 'What is her name?'

He smiled charmingly at me. 'This is Minstrel, Lady Grace,' he told me. 'She is the best horse I have ever ridden. She is from Spain and has Andalusian blood.'

'Then she is valuable indeed,' I gasped, 'for I know that Andalusians are amongst the most prized of horses.'

'Do you not wish to be at the head of the hunt?' asked Lord Ruxbury.

'I have no taste for the kill, my lord,' I replied. 'And in truth I am a poor horsewoman.' I was sure that my companion was going to laugh at me – and indeed it had taken some courage to admit my failings.

But Lord Ruxbury did not mock me. 'I doubt that you are a poor horsewoman,' he said, as if in disbelief, 'for you have a good seat.'

'I may look well in the saddle while Doucette walks,' I laughed, 'but wait until she decides to canter!'

Just then we were nearly joined by Mr Naunton. I say 'nearly' because, as he trotted towards our party, his horse stumbled a little and he was thrown forwards. Looking terrified, he clung to the horse's neck to keep himself in the saddle, at which the horse took fright and galloped off!

'Mr Naunton seems to be in haste to find the prey!' Lord Ruxbury remarked solemnly. I swear I tried to keep my countenance, but I could not stop myself from laughing. Everyone else joined in, apart from Lady Jane, who gave us all a very cold stare. We watched as Mr Naunton was carried away into the distance and finally shaken off into a ditch.

'Poor Mr Naunton,' sighed Lord Ruxbury.

Poor Mr Naunton indeed, I thought. He has proved himself to be a very poor horseman, just like the felons described by the drunkard! And it had not escaped me that his horse was black as jet.

But I had no time to pursue this thought, for Lord Ruxbury was addressing us again. 'I have the greatest sympathy for Mr Naunton,' he was saying earnestly. 'It is so hard to keep one's seat on an excitable steed. I myself have a deal of trouble.'

I was astounded at his words. Surely he had already proved his skill. Yet even as he spoke Minstrel reared up, pawing the air with her hooves, and then began to canter round us, bucking all the while. Lord Ruxbury did not seem to be able to master her at all. Then his mare suddenly changed course and headed straight for the trees. She galloped under a low hanging branch, knocking her rider clean out of the saddle, and stopped a little way off to munch some grass. Lord Ruxbury dangled from the branch, kicking his legs wildly, trying to swing up into the tree but slipping each time. I wished at that moment that I was a better horsewoman, so I could have ridden to his rescue. But I soon saw that there was no need, for Lord Ruxbury was merely playing the fool! He gave a whistle, and Minstrel dutifully stopped munching and backed up until she was underneath him. Her master dropped lightly down into the saddle. We all applauded.

'I have never seen such skill!' laughed Mary Shelton. 'And from so handsome a gentleman!' she added under her breath.

'Indeed,' added Lady Sarah. 'If it were not for Sir Roger . . .'

Lord Ruxbury rode back to us and we all prepared to ride on. But as I gathered my reins, I dropped my crop. In a flash, Lord Ruxbury had dismounted, swept up the crop and presented it back to me with a bow – and a smile. Then he backed a good ten paces from Minstrel's hindquarters, ran full pelt towards her, leaped and vaulted straight into the saddle! We all gasped in wonder and applauded louder than ever. I do not think any of us had ever seen such horsemanship. Lord Ruxbury smiled and made some elegant bows. His clever clowning puts me in mind of Masou. He too knows how to woo and frighten his audience at the same time.

I came out of my reverie and suddenly realized that the other Maids had trotted on ahead and Lord Ruxbury was speaking to me.

'I believe that lunch will be laid out at Ox Pond,' he was saying. 'There is Snow Hill yonder. We just have time to canter up it. Will you join me, as it seems our party has forsaken us?'

I was about to beg to be excused when he sprang from his saddle and took Doucette's bridle.

'Do not fear the canter, my lady,' he smiled. 'Allow me to offer you Minstrel as your mount and in return I shall ride Doucette.'

'But, my lord,' I protested, 'I have neither the skill nor the confidence for such a fine animal!'

'Minstrel is fine indeed,' agreed Lord Ruxbury, 'and bright and quick to learn. Yet for all that she is the most gentle of horses. She would be an ideal mount. A well-schooled horse can teach its rider much.' He helped me as I reluctantly dismounted from Doucette.

'But Minstrel's saddle will not do for me,

sir,' I protested, pleased to have found an excuse not to change horses. 'I need a side-saddle.'

I can admit here in my daybooke that I would feel safer riding a horse in the same way as a man does, with one leg either side, but that would not do for one of Her Majesty's Maids of Honour.

But my companion was determined to have his way!

'Fie, Lady Grace,' he said, as he undid Minstrel's girth. 'Saddles can be swapped in an instant. Doucette and Minstrel are not so very different in size as to make the task impossible.'

He was right. In a moment he had deftly secured my saddle onto Minstrel's back and helped me to mount. When he had adjusted Minstrel's girth and saddled up Doucette, he jumped onto her. Poor Doucette was not used to so much activity and looked as if she wanted to throw him off. But Lord Ruxbury gave her one smart tap with his whip to show her who was master and she thought better of it. I wished I could do that.

'If you will allow a little tutelage before we set off, my lady,' said Lord Ruxbury, 'I think we shall make great progress. Minstrel responds to the lightest of touches and has a very soft mouth – thus she will obey your slightest signal.'

Not when she finds out how poor a rider I am, I thought mournfully. But there was nothing for it. I gathered up the reins and brushed Minstrel's side with my leg. I did not expect anything to happen. Doucette would certainly not have responded to such a movement. But to my astonishment Minstrel went instantly into a walk! I touched her side again and she moved forwards into a comfortable trot!

Sitting deep in the saddle as Lord Ruxbury instructed, I was soon cantering up the hill and feeling as if I could fly! I had never thought that riding could be so enjoyable. I vow here and now to have an Andalusian horse of my own one day.

We came to a halt at the top of the hill. I was glad that there were other courtiers there, for I realized that I had been unchaperoned for a while! Scandalous!

'Expertly ridden, Lady Grace!' exclaimed Lord Ruxbury. 'I have never yet had a more ready pupil!'

'I think the credit must go more to the tutor than the student, sir,' I replied when I had recovered my breath, although to tell the truth I was proud of my performance.

From here we could see the leaders of the hunt following the greyhounds across the Heybourne Walk.

'I am content that it is you who are under my tutelage,' said my companion as we watched them. 'There are many at Court whom it would be most irksome to teach! Imagine old Mr Tuppins, whom I have ofttimes seen drunk.' Lord Ruxbury wobbled in his saddle in a wonderful imitation. '*I cannot sheem to get me feet in the shtirrups, shir . . . and where'sh the horshe gone?*'

I burst out laughing. 'That is Mr Tuppins to the life!' I gasped.

'And what if your worthy Mistress

Champernowne were here?' he went on. 'I saw her but yesterday chiding Mr Secretary Cecil for dropping egg on his doublet. I doubt she would keep her thoughts on the riding for an instant. *Never mind my seat, Lord Ruxbury*, she would say, *what about that mud on your boots, look you? Never have I seen such a sight. Hie you to the castle now and put on some clean ones!*'

Lord Ruxbury is truly a wonderful mimic. I had been so well entertained that I had quite forgotten about Mr Naunton and the theft.

As we moved forwards to join the other Maids, I saw that Mr Naunton was now riding alongside Lady Jane. I had a good stare at him to appease my conscience, and tried to picture him as a brigand. It was not easy! He looked as if he would as likely journey to the moon as dare to steal Her Majesty's gold. Yet he met the description of the felon – his horse was entirely black, and he was a poor horseman. I decided to try and find out more about him later. There were too many distractions at the hunt.

I think it may be time for supper now – if

my growling stomach is right. I shall go there directly.

Oh, I nearly forgot! As we returned to the castle, a figure on a black horse burst out from the trees, shot across our path and ploughed into a bush on the other side with a terrified cry. It was Mr Naunton again!

In the Presence Chamber, late

The other Maids have gone to their beds and I should have done so too. But tomorrow I shall be about the Queen's secret business at first light and shall have no time to make an entry. Although it is so late and my eyelids are drooping with tiredness, I have sneaked into the empty Presence Chamber and slipped behind an arras with a candle to write. Now I am seated on the floor and must remember to keep the flame away from the tapestry that hides me.

The Queen had ordered a sumptuous feast

and dancing for this evening in honour of Penelope and her family. Her Majesty was dressed tonight in her white and gold gown, the sleeves and bodice wrought all over with spangles. As always she looked magnificent.

I knew that the best way for me to find out more about Mr Naunton was to dance all evening. It was worth the aching feet, for I was able to glean scraps of information from my partners. I soon learned that my suspect is known to be a keen gambler, whatever Lady Jane says, but not a very good one, for he often loses. One courtier did tell me that Mr Naunton had lately come into a large sum of money, but he had no idea how.

As the musicians struck up a Pavane, I found myself partnered by Mr Hatton. This was a great honour, for everyone knows he is the best dancer at Court. Unfortunately, I could not enjoy it as I usually would, for my head was full of the mystery. This was a perfect opportunity to learn what Mr Hatton knew of the thieves. I brought the subject round to the robbery as if it had just entered my thoughts.

'Have you caught your thieves yet, Mr Hatton?' I enquired as we walked along the line of dancers. 'For Lady Sarah has had her new necklace and all her precious jewels locked up every night in a chest within a chest!'

This was not true, but as Mr Hatton would not be coming into our bedchamber I thought I was on safe ground.

'I can assure all the Maids of Honour that they are perfectly secure within the castle,' he replied with a kind smile. 'The felons are just forest bandits and likely to be lurking there still. My men will find them, I have no doubt.'

I had no time to ask any more, for at that moment we were interrupted by one of the Gentlemen of the Guard. He looked travel-stained and most eager to speak with Mr Hatton.

'By your leave, my lady,' said Mr Hatton with a bow, 'I must reluctantly attend to this matter. It pertains to the very subject of which we were talking.'

I wonder what he would have said if I had refused him leave and insisted we finished the

Pavane! But in truth I was as anxious as my partner to learn what the guard had to say. I nodded and stepped back. But I did not go far. I suddenly found that a bow on my sleeve needed urgent attention and I had to stop – within earshot.

'I have come post-haste from Meadowfold, sir,' said the messenger in a low voice. 'There is a boy in the village who has knowledge of the thief at the inn.'

'Indeed,' replied Mr Hatton briskly. 'What does he know?'

'He came upon the man escaping, sir,' the messenger told him. 'It seems that he had some speech with him.'

'Then I will ride to Meadowfold tomorrow at first light and see the lad,' said Mr Hatton. 'You have done well, Mr Drummond. You are weary with your travelling. Rest up and I will have you with me on the morrow.'

'I will, sir,' answered the guard, looking relieved that he did not have to face another ride so soon.

'But first, get you to the other guards,'

instructed Mr Hatton. 'I would have one of them journey directly to Meadowfold and make the boy ready for my early arrival on the morrow. I will go to Her Majesty forth-with and tell her this news.'

'Lady Grace,' said a voice in my ear, 'you are without a partner. How can this be?'

I had been too intent on listening to the conversation to notice anyone approaching me. I spun round. It was Lord Ruxbury.

'I believe there is to be a Volta next,' he said with a bow, 'and I would be honoured if you would dance it with me.'

'And I know why, my lord,' I answered with a smile. 'I am lighter than most ladies here and easier to lift.'

'How can you reason thus?' said Lord Ruxbury in mock horror as he led me to join the line. 'Although I would as soon take the floor with a sack of flour as try to haul Lady Scudamore off the ground!'

I giggled at this. Lady Scudamore is rather portly.

My Lord Ruxbury is an excellent dancer,

and he lifted me up as if I were as light as a feather. When the Queen is dancing, no gentleman dare lift his partner as high as Her Majesty. But the Queen was deep in conversation with Mr Hatton so I felt as if my head would touch the ceiling!

We then danced a stately Almain. In truth I was glad to get my breath back. Although I was enjoying myself, I began to think about the boy at Meadowfold. I realized that I needed to hear his story for myself. After all, how else would I find out exactly what the lad had to say? Perhaps if I went to the Queen, she would allow me to go with Mr Hatton on the morrow. Suddenly Lord Ruxbury interrupted my musings.

'How now, Lady Grace,' he said. 'Why the solemn look? I know I am no match for Mr Hatton at the dance, but I did not think myself so poor. I trust it was nothing but the most serious matter that took such a fine dancer from your side.'

'Have no fear, my lord,' I assured him with a smile. 'Your dancing pleases me well. Mr

Hatton was called away on the matter of a witness to the theft of the Queen's gold. He is going to Meadowfold at first light.'

'That is good news indeed!' exclaimed Lord Ruxbury. 'We can but hope that the brigands will soon be under lock and key.'

'And yet I am not convinced that it was brigands who made off with the gold,' I said, as we slip-stepped up the hall. 'I have a suspicion that the thief may even be someone here at Court.' Lord Ruxbury raised an eyebrow at this but he did not laugh at me and I felt encouraged to continue. 'Tell me, Lord Ruxbury, what know you of Mr Naunton?'

'I hear he is a fine poet,' replied my partner, with a twinkle in his eye.

'But what of his skill at cards?' I persisted. 'He seems an unlucky gambler to me.'

Lord Ruxbury made an elaborate show of making sure that no one was within earshot. 'Aye, my lady,' he whispered. 'Mr Naunton places large and risky bets and seldom wins – though he has been telling all and sundry that he has just won a goodly wager.'

'Do not tell Lady Jane,' I cautioned him as we finished the honour at the end of the dance. 'He has convinced her that he is no gambler!'

'But is he your main suspect?' asked Lord Ruxbury, leading me to the side of the hall. 'He does not look like a thief. He is surely better suited to rhyme than robbery. Have you considered Mr Layton? He has a shifty look.' Lord Ruxbury narrowed his eyes in imitation. I laughed. He knows full well that poor Mr Layton has a squint and cannot help his looks, shifty or otherwise. 'No,' Lord Ruxbury went on, making his voice whine just like Mr Layton's, 'he is too puny to take on the might of the Gentlemen of the Guard.' He stroked his beard, pretending to think hard about the problem. 'Then what of Lord Coldicott?' he suggested, grinning wickedly. 'He has recently come into a fortune and is said to drink with the ne'er-do-wells of Windsor village. Two of them could have been his accomplices. However, I think not. He often has trouble finding his way about the castle and could hardly have outwitted Mr Hatton's men.'

'Why do you not offer your thoughts to Her Majesty?' I laughed. 'They are so entertaining she would have you take Mr Somers's place as Queen's Fool!'

'Cruel Lady Grace!' exclaimed Lord Ruxbury, his hand on his heart. 'How can you mock my deliberations? Now do not stop my train of thought. I have heard there were three horsemen. Mayhap they are all at Court. Though if it were just one man he could have all the treasure to himself. A lone thief would be a happy thief indeed.'

'I have it!' I declared. 'It is portly old Sir Pelham Poucher. He is so wide that he could look like three men all at once!'

A few minutes later

I had to stop writing, for I heard footsteps moving across the Presence Chamber just the other side of my curtain. I have quickly thought up an excuse for being here if I am discovered. I will say that I was so tired after the dancing I sat for a moment behind this arras and must have fallen asleep. (Hopefully they will not notice the daybooke on my lap – or the candle!) Luckily the footsteps have now moved away and are fading from my hearing.

Lord Ruxbury then asked if I would not like to assist Mr Hatton with his investigation, as I seemed to be taking quite an interest in the theft.

I suddenly realized I had been enjoying our game so much that I had lowered my guard and perhaps told him more than I should. I must not give away my secret office for the Queen.

'Oh no,' I gabbled, trying to sound as empty-headed as Lady Sarah when she is playing the helpless woman. 'It is just a game between us. For who am I to worry about such things? No, I am sure that the Gentlemen of the Guard will catch the robbers with no help from me.

I am a mere Maid of Honour, not one of Mr Hatton's men.'

'I am truly thankful that you are not a man, my lady!' Lord Ruxbury said gallantly.

I was surprised to find that my cheeks felt hot, but the room was very warm. 'You are most kind, Lord Ruxbury,' I mumbled. 'But now, please excuse me, for I must attend the Queen.'

I scuttled off quickly. I was telling the truth, for I did wish to seek an audience with Her Majesty. I needed her permission to go with Mr Hatton to Meadowfold.

If I had been a young courtier ready to flatter Her Majesty I would have gained her attention immediately. But I could not get through the throng of fawning men trying to out-grovel each other with their flattery. The things the Queen was compared to: the finest diamond, the beautiful shimmer of moonlight on a lake, the fattest sow in the sty. In truth I made the last one up, but the comparisons were getting sillier and sillier. However, Her Majesty was lapping up the compliments like a cat with cream and seemed to want nothing to do with a Maid of Honour who would have no pretty words for her.

It was not until she had retired to her bedchamber that I succeeded in speaking to her.

'What is it, Grace, that keeps you from your rest?' asked the Queen, when she had dismissed her servant. She was wearing a lace bed gown. She handed me an ivory comb and I made myself useful attending to her long fiery tresses. She was in a fine humour and I was grateful to her courtly flatterers. 'It can hardly be about my stolen gold, for Mr Hatton has assured me that matters progress well. It seems he has another witness that may lead him to the felons. I am happy to say that there is nothing for my Lady Pursuivant to do.'

'I fear there may be, My Liege,' I said a little nervously. It is not wise to contradict Her Majesty even when she is in a good humour. I carried on quickly. 'With your permission I would accompany Mr Hatton to Meadowfold on the morrow, and see his witness for myself.'

'Impossible!' said the Queen, shaking her head so hard that I got the comb tangled in her hair! 'I wish my god-daughter safe. That is why you were to keep your activities within the environs of the castle.'

I knew Her Majesty was concerned only for my welfare, but I felt sure that the investigation depended upon my being there to hear the boy. I wondered how I could soothe her fears – and get the comb free without her knowing.

'Gracious Queen,' I said humbly, as I wriggled the comb a little, 'let me be your eyes and ears in Meadowfold. Be assured I shall be safe under Mr Hatton's protection, and perchance the boy will talk more openly to me, who is nearer to his age. I warrant he will be tongue-tied in the presence of the Gentlemen of the Guard, and especially Mr Hatton.'

The Queen threw back her head and laughed. To my relief, the comb came free or I would have pulled out a large tuft of the royal hair.

'How can I refuse one who argues so cleverly?' she said. 'I will tell Mr Hatton that you are to go with him. But he must not guess the real reason. Let me consider awhile . . .' She rose and walked about her chamber. 'I have it!' she said finally. 'If I mistake not there is a certain farmer at Meadowfold who grows excellent vegetables, and I have a sudden yearning for early asparagus at the wedding feast! The Gentlemen of the Guard may feel it a petty matter to be fetching food for me, so you must do it.'

I smiled. Her Majesty and I knew well enough that her Gentlemen of the Guard, and especially Mr Hatton, would go to the ends of the earth to fetch a single pea if she desired it!

'Yet I have a condition, Grace,' she went on. 'I would have you take Mary Shelton with you. She is steady and will keep you from mischief.' She caught sight of herself in her looking glass. 'You have made a veritable bird's nest of my hair, Grace!' she exclaimed. I hurried forward with the comb. 'No, indeed,' she smiled, taking it from me. 'I trust you have better skill at untangling this mystery.'

So I am off to Meadowfold in the morning. In just a few hours, in truth! I must away to bed. Hell's teeth! I have forgotten to tell Mary Shelton the Queen's orders. I fear she may already be asleep!

The Twenty-third Day of April, in the Year of Our Lord 1570

St George's Day!

It is the day of Penelope and Thomas's wedding! At four of the clock, in only an hour and a half's time, the Court will gather at St George's Chapel to see them married. I am dressed and ready and very excited, but this crime is like wool that a kitten has been at – it is almost impossible to unravel!

I am tucked in the corner of my chamber, trying to write about what happened this morning. I must order my thoughts and forget for a moment the festivities to come. That is if I can ignore all the squealing from Lady Sarah as Olwen ties her sleeves on. They look fine to me but do not seem to satisfy my fussy lady. Fran is quietly helping Mary Shelton into her farthingale.

I am dressed already and I have to admit

my new yellow gown is lovely – although Fran has tied me into my bumroll and corset so tightly that I feel like a trussed chicken. At least, if Mrs Champernowne comes in, she cannot chide me, for I am completely ready. Except she is likely to fuss that I will get ink on my dress! Penelope will never forgive me if I appear at the wedding with black spots. Nor would the Queen!

Now I have fetched the black satin apron that the Queen gave me, so my dress should be safe.

Anyway, last night I had to pluck up my courage to wake Mary Shelton. She was not a little cross at being woken from a deep sleep to be told that she would be woken again at crack of dawn the next morning! Yet I do admire her. She did not ask me any questions when I told her that our mission was merely to collect asparagus – she knows that I only ask for her help when I really need it.

I left a note for Lady Sarah to tell Mrs Champernowne that Mary and I had gone in search of asparagus on the Queen's orders, and

I was about to make myself ready for bed when a thought suddenly struck me. How could I be sure of waking before sunrise? Then I had a wonderful idea. Poor Ellie is well used to being up at first light. Indeed, she often grumbles about having to light the fires under the coppers 'before Mrs Fadget has poked her ugly old nose from her bedclothes'. I felt guilty about giving her the extra task of waking us, but it would be a chance to reward her with some money (she is too proud to accept coins for nothing) and I know that she is always most eager to help the Queen's Lady Pursuivant. So I crept down to the laundry, where Ellie was still hard at work.

Her eyes sparkled with the thought of the adventure. 'Of course I'll wake you, Grace,' she said. 'But can't I come too? 'Twould not be the first time I've helped you in Her Majesty's service. And I could don some fine clothes for the purpose!'

'Not this time, Ellie,' I said gently, trying not to smile at her hopeful expression. 'I have only just succeeded in persuading the Queen to let me go.' Ellie looked crestfallen. 'But I promise to tell you every detail when I return.'

She brightened at that, and when I pressed some coins into her hand she exclaimed, 'I'll get a pasty as big as me 'ead with these!'

When Ellie shook Mary and me awake this morning I thought it was still the middle of the night and she had played some trick on us. I groaned out loud. Lady Sarah stirred at that and we all held our breath. But she soon turned over and began to murmur in her sleep about some gentleman or other. And I don't think it was Sir Roger! Ellie stuffed a corner of my sheet in her mouth to stifle her giggles.

'Hush, Ellie!' I hissed, although I wanted to laugh myself. 'What time is it?'

'The chapel clock has not long chimed five,' Ellie whispered, when she had recovered her breath. 'You'd better hurry.'

'Thank you, Ellie,' I whispered, wishing she could come with me.

'I hope you find all the asparagus you need,' she said, winking at me behind Mary's back.

'Now, I must be about my work.' She slipped silently out of the door.

Mary and I struggled into our clothes by the dim dawn light, helping each other with our lacing. We put on our cloaks and crept down to the Engine Court, where Henry Westerland was waiting to escort us to the stables. We were to mount our horses there, for we did not want to wake anyone – especially the Queen. There was a little light in the sky but we were grateful for the torches that lit our way down the slope and past the chapel.

When we arrived at the stables I could see that Mr Hatton was displeased at having to ride with two Maids. I heard him bemoaning our presence to one of his men. 'They will doubtless slow our pace,' he was saying.

'What are we to do?' Mary Shelton whispered to me. 'I do not wish to upset Mr Hatton, and yet we must go, on the Queen's orders.'

'Leave this to me, Mary,' I said. I walked up to Mr Hatton. 'You are most kind, sir,' I gushed, 'to have agreed to our accompanying you thus.'

I knew he had no choice in the matter, but I find that a little flattery often helps. 'May I assure you that Mary Shelton and I will match your pace. My companion is a good horse-woman and I have been taking lessons from one of the best riders at Court.'

I admit it was rash of me to promise to match the pace, but it brought a smile to Mr Hatton's face. It was fortunate he did not know that the only occasion I have had any tutor-ing lately was yesterday with Lord Ruxbury at the hunt! But the journey was steady, we travelled on quite good roads and, much to my relief, Doucette avoided stumbling in the holes and unseating me.

In truth the three hours passed pleasantly enough. Unlike their master, the four Gentle-men of the Guard who rode with us were pleased to have Maids of Honour for company. (Although I am sure they would have preferred Lady Sarah with her heaving bosom and Lady Jane with her fluttering eyelashes!)

There was a good deal of joking and showing off, to which nearly all young men seem prone whenever ladies are within earshot. Then, when I least expected it, I found out something important. We had just slowed to a walk after cantering a while, and I was trying to get my breath back – although I was pleased that I had not once felt I might slip from the saddle.

'I heard you were made a goose of the day before yesterday, Edward,' Harry Thornham was saying to the guard who rode alongside him.

'It was a private matter between two gentlemen,' the other replied, looking rather embarrassed.

'Private?' guffawed Samuel Twyer from behind. 'You were letting the whole world know about it when you first made that wager with Mr Naunton!'

My ears pricked up at the name. I turned my head to hear better and nearly slipped off my saddle into a ditch. (I should not have been so pleased with my skill in the canter. It is true that pride comes before a fall!)

''Twas a right foolish wager too!' Mr Hatton

said, joining in the fun with a wink at Mary and me. 'Who in their senses would bet that a goose could run faster than a dog?'

'Edward was in his cups,' laughed Samuel Twyer, 'and a drunken man will say many a doltish thing.'

'I would that I had seen your face, Edward, when the dog won the race!' said Hugh Morling.

'Was it a large wager?' I asked.

'It was a handsome sum, my lady,' replied Mr Hatton. 'I think you could say that Mr Naunton came into a fortune that day.'

Hell's teeth! It seemed unlikely that Mr Naunton was the thief. He had won his money publicly, in a wager, and that was how he had repaid Sir Roger Spratling.

I confess I felt most despondent. Who else could the villain be? I had been so sure it must be Mr Naunton – although I was glad for Lady Jane's sake that he was not the man. I had led myself on a wild goose chase, I thought, and then I could not help but smile at my poor choice of metaphor.

My only hope now was that the boy at

Meadowfold might throw some light on this dark matter. Perhaps Mr Hatton was right and the men were common brigands after all. If so, I hoped the boy's words would make it certain, so that I could rid myself of this strange conviction that the theft was the work of a courtier.

Then I grew fanciful. Mayhap the thieves were sturdy beggars, but even they would not be safe from the Queen's Lady Pursuivant if she had a fast steed and purpose in her heart. If only I were an accomplished rider with Minstrel as my mount, I mused, then I could gallop like the wind in pursuit, catch the felons and bring them cringing before the Queen. But I decided that it would probably be more fun if I took Lord Ruxbury with me, as well as his horse – but only because he is a good horseman and excellent company.

'Grace!' came Mary Shelton's voice. 'You must be daydreaming. You are smiling at the air!'

'I was just thinking of . . . of asparagus,' I told her, going a little pink. After all, I could not explain that my mind had been on my secret investigations.

'Mr Hatton tells me that we are nearly arrived,' said Mary. 'The inn is in the middle of the village.'

And indeed, I could see the smoke rising from the chimneys of Meadowfold a little further along the way. We had now reached a crossroads. I thought it must be the very place where the thieves had been seen by the drunkard. I tried to get my bearings. Ahead of us was the road to Portsmouth, and to our left I could see Windsor Forest in the distance. That was the direction the drunken man had said the brigands took. Our party turned right and entered the village.

I was wondering how I could contrive to speak with the boy Mr Hatton had come to see, when we rounded a corner and stopped under a large oak tree. We were outside a rambling old building with a battered wooden board hanging from a branch. On it was a picture of what was supposed to be a black cat – although it looked more like an elderly weasel to me. This had to be the Black Cat Inn! We had arrived at the place where the robbery had occurred, and I felt my heartbeat quicken. Surely there would be some clue here that would lead me to the true thieves.

But I could go no further with my investigation, for Mr Hatton leaped from his horse.

'Mr Bainbridge,' he said, 'accompany these two ladies to the house of the asparagus grower yonder.'

I caught Edward Bainbridge giving a triumphant look to his companions – I suppose because he had been chosen as our escort, while the others had to stand guard outside the inn.

We were helped to dismount. Then Edward Bainbridge strode proudly off down the road and we had no choice but to follow him. As we went I looked back and saw Mr Hatton knocking loudly on the door of the inn. I felt sorry for the lad who must be waiting for him inside. Mr Hatton is a good man, but can sound rather stern and frightening when he is about the Queen's business. I decided we should get back to the inn as quickly as possible so that I might have a chance to speak to the boy.

'Hurry, Mary,' I called. 'We must hasten to the farm, else . . . else the asparagus may spoil!'

However, fortune was not with me. The asparagus grower's wife wanted to talk and talk and talk!

'This is such an honour, your ladyships!' she gushed, as she curtsied deeply before us. 'Do forgive me,' she added, struggling to get herself upright again. 'It's just my knees. Of late they won't do as I tell them. Not that you fine ladies want to know about my problems, I'm sure.' She showed Mary and me into a small room where a scrawny, grey-haired man stood nervously grasping a basket piled high with fresh green asparagus. 'This is my husband, Amos Butts,' she explained. As Mr Butts seemed paralysed with fright, his wife took the basket and held it out to us. Then she suddenly put it down again.

'Fancy our Most Gracious Sovereign honouring us in this way, Amos!' she exclaimed. 'What do you think of that?' She didn't wait for a reply but went straight on. 'In truth, my ladies, my husband does have a wonderful gift with the asparagus, as with everything he grows, although I say it as shouldn't. If Her Majesty thinks fit she could send for some of his strawberries later in the year – and of course you must take his finest rhubarb with you now. I have put some in the bottom of the basket. There is nothing so tasty as a compote of rhubarb . . .'

I wanted to grab the basket and escape! I think Mary could sense my agitation, for she came to my rescue.

'You are most kind, Mistress Butts,' she said, with a smile. 'And in return I shall send you a soothing poultice which is sure to help with your joints. It has been most effective in easing the pain of the rheumatics in Lady Knollys's ankle and may do the same for your knees.'

'I am deeply thankful to you, my lady, for taking such trouble,' Mistress Butts sighed in delight. 'To think I have the same complaint as a high-born lady!' She seemed almost pleased with her bad knees if it meant she was to be treated like nobility! Mercifully the thought of Mary's kindness now seemed to have rendered her as speechless as her husband. She silently handed over the basket and took the purse of money that Mary gave her. We were about to leave, but then Mr Butts found his tongue! I could have screamed with frustration.

'Is my sparrowgrass truly for Her Majesty?' he muttered, staring at his boots.

'Yes, indeed,' said Mary. 'The Queen said she would have no asparagus but yours, Farmer Butts.'

Mr Butts blushed as red as the beetroot that I am sure he also grows. However, he seemed to have used up all his words, for he said no more and at last we were able to take our leave.

We rejoined Edward Bainbridge, who was waiting in the road outside.

'We must hurry,' I said, and I set off back to the inn as fast as I could walk. 'I do not want to be too late to . . . I mean, I do not wish to delay Mr Hatton.'

'Slow down a little,' panted Mary, trying to keep up with me. 'Whatever the reason for your haste, I think you will be much better served by not being out of breath!'

As we entered the inn, we could see an open door leading into a private room. Mr Hatton sat there at a table looking very important. He was just dismissing a young boy of about eight. The boy swaggered out; obviously Mr Hatton had not frightened him. I desperately wanted to know what they had discussed, and I was just wondering how I could find out, when Mr Hatton demanded to speak with one of the serving maids, which gave me a little time to talk to the boy! I hoped it would be enough.

Unfortunately, our escort was hovering near us. I certainly did not want him spying on me, but he was determined to be a most loyal body-guard to us − even within the safety of the inn. (I think his companions could see him through the window.)

I took Mary Shelton's arm and led her aside. 'You would do me a great service if you would take our "shadow" and keep him busy for a while,' I whispered.

Mary smiled knowingly. 'I have an uncommon thirst!' she said aloud. 'Mr Bainbridge, would you be so kind as to order some refreshment for me?' At that I realized that I had eaten nothing since last night. It is a measure of my loyalty to the Queen that I resisted the temptation to join them.

'At once, my lady,' said the guard happily. When he had given his orders to the innkeeper, Mary invited him to join her in a quiet corner of the inn. He could hardly disguise his delight. I was surprised he did not knock on the window to make certain that the others knew of his luck.

As soon as they were seated I slipped out into the passage and caught up with the young boy. If he was surprised that a fine lady wished to speak to him, he made no sign. I imagine that he was feeling rather important after talking to the leader of the Queen's Gentlemen of the Guard.

'Wait a minute, young sir,' I said. 'Her Majesty

is sure to want to know what service you performed for her, and I wish to tell her I had it from your own lips.'

Now he did look impressed. 'You will speak to the Queen about me?' he gasped.

I nodded. 'And she will be most pleased with you, for I believe you have done your duty to her.'

'That I have, or my name's not Seth Shearsmith!' he declared proudly, puffing out his puny chest. 'I told the gentleman everything I saw three nights ago.'

'And that was . . . ?' I prompted him. I knew I did not have much time, for soon someone would realize I was unattended.

'It were very early in the morning,' said Seth, 'and I shouldn't have been out of bed, but I couldn't find Sidney — he's my pet rat — and then I found him by the ale casks at the back of the inn. He'd supped a bit too much, for he'd gone most wobbly.'

'And what did you see?' I asked — though 'twas a shame, for I should have liked to hear more about Sidney.

'Oh, my lady,' he exclaimed. 'First I saw a big black horse waiting. It was a cold night and I could see its breath in the light from my lantern. Then a man appeared at an upper window and I thought I was seeing a ghost, for he was tall and all in black as well. He was carrying two big saddlebags. He climbed down onto one of the casks, and then he jumped to the ground and made to go for his horse. He almost knocked me over! I stood as still as a stone. I didn't know what to do. This man is up to no good, I sez to myself, and I thought I might have to fight him! Then he held a finger up to his lips and I knew he wanted me to keep quiet, so I did.'

'You are certain there was only one man and one horse?' I enquired.

'Aye, my lady.' He nodded firmly. 'No one else was about at all but me, and the man in black.'

'And did you see his face?' I asked.

'No, my lady,' Seth replied. 'He had a kerchief over his nose and mouth so I could only see his eyes in the lantern light and they were right merry. O' course, if I'd had the chance I would have unmasked him,' he added boldly.

I guessed that this was not true, and he was more likely to have run away given the opportunity! But I think he was like many young boys, and dreamed of being a hero.

'What happened then?' I queried. Thus far, the boy's story had given me no new clues as to the thief's identity.

'Me and Sidney must have scared 'im off,' Seth told me, 'because he buckled the bags onto his saddle in a flash and then he jumped right quickly upon his horse – and with a trick I've never seen before. He did not put his foot in the stirrups like any other man. He leaped onto it from behind! I was right impressed by that, and I mean to learn how to do it. I could and all, for my pony is not tall and I could start with that and . . .'

He gabbled on but I was too shocked to listen. I knew of only one man who could mount a horse in that way.

In the North-east Tower

I have run up here to the tower as I could not stay in my chamber a moment longer! A page knocked at the door and told Olwen that Mrs Champernowne was expecting us in her parlour. She wished to read us something quiet and improving to make us ready for the solemn ceremony. I knew she would not put up with me scratching away at my daybooke, and I still have so much to write!

So, back to Seth and the masked robber. The only man I knew who could mount a horse the way the boy had described was Lord Ruxbury! But it couldn't possibly be him, I realized. He would not have had time to play cards until nearly two in the morning, ride all the way to Meadowfold and back, and then appear in the Great Kitchen before sunrise. That would have given him only a little more than three hours to complete the whole task.

Surely even the swiftest horse could not journey so far in so little time. And yet Lord Ruxbury does have one of the best horses I have ever seen. I did not know what to think. I resolved to investigate further.

'Tell me, Seth,' I said anxiously. 'I have heard that the horse the thief rode was black. Did it have a white blaze on its nose?'

'No, indeed, my lady,' said Seth, shaking his head. 'It were pure black.'

'Are you certain?' I asked.

'Yes, my lady!' he answered vehemently. 'I saw it clearly. It were a fine horse though.'

Well, I knew it was unlikely that Lord Ruxbury was the robber. Minstrel is the finest horse I have ever seen and has been much admired at Court, but she has a bright white blaze and white socks that are unmistakable, while the horse Seth saw was pure black. I realized that it was more likely someone else had learned Lord Ruxbury's clever trick of vaulting onto a horse.

Suddenly there was a commotion outside, and I heard Mr Hatton called for. I did not want someone to come and find me without an escort, so I thanked Seth, gave him a coin from my purse and went to see what the fuss was about.

There was a stooped old man at the door of the inn ranting at Henry Westerland. He was shabbily dressed and carried a sack in one grimy hand. Even from where I stood, I could smell that his clothes and his person had not been washed for many a day.

'What is all this?' demanded Mr Hatton.

'Are you the Captain?' asked the old man, squinting at him. 'I 'eard you was looking for some thieves. Well, I got a complaint that you might like to 'ear.' He rubbed his grimy fingers as if suggesting some coins might help his memory, but Mr Hatton ignored this.

'Speak, man!' he ordered. 'I command you in the name of Her Gracious Majesty, Queen Elizabeth.'

'Of course, o noble lordship,' simpered the man, 'for a truer subject of Her Majesty than me you will never find. I 'ave a pig farm close to the Windsor road, and I want you to find the scoundrels 'oo slept in my barn three nights ago!' The old man had a complaining whine to his voice. He scratched at his breeches and we all stepped back for fear of catching a flea.

'This sounds like a local matter,' said Mr Hatton impatiently. 'I am too busy for—'

'But that was the very same night as the robbery!' I gasped breathlessly, pretending to be the silly Maid.

'The very same, your ladyship,' nodded the strange old man. 'You're sharp, and no mistake!'

'Are you certain this happened three nights since?' demanded Mr Hatton.

'As sure as the eggs my chickens would 'ave laid if they 'adn't been scared away on account of my unwanted visitors,' croaked the old man. 'Clucking and squawking, they were. I thought a fox 'ad got in among them but there were no sign of old Reynard. It were 'oomans what disturbed them and chased 'em away. Now, my Bessie were the best layer I ever 'ad and I've not seen 'er nor the others from that day to this. It's not right. I'm a God-fearing man, I am.'

At last he had to draw breath and Mr Hatton was able to speak.

'It could have been any band of ruffians, my good man,' he said sternly.

'You'll not say that when you see what I found!' The old man gave a grin, showing his rotten teeth. Then he delved into his sack, and the Gentlemen of the Guard raised their swords as he pulled out an ivory-handled wheel-lock pistol!

'That is the gun!' exclaimed Hugh Morling. 'The very gun the thief pointed at my heart!'

'Then we must search the barn without delay,' declared Mr Hatton, taking the gun and signalling to his men.

''Tis not far up the road,' said the old pig farmer. 'I'll lead you there.'

I was determined to go as well, and I did not wish to give Mr Hatton a chance to decide otherwise, so I pulled at his sleeve. 'You will not be leaving Mary Shelton and me here without protection, Mr Hatton,' I said, trying to sound a little like the Queen. 'We shall accompany you.'

Mr Hatton nodded, and without more ado we were all mounted and riding back to the crossroads. We turned onto the Windsor road, but almost at once left it and took a rutted track. The old man, who was muttering and cursing all chicken chasers, walked ahead of us.

Before long we reached the pig farm itself. We could see the forest beyond it. The thieves could have made for the forest and then doubled back across the fields to cover their trail.

The pig farm was a mess. There was a tiny house of sorts and a group of ramshackle barns beyond. The buildings did not deserve such a name, for they were just planks of rotten wood leaning against each other. We dismounted and the farmer led us inside one of the barns. The door was broken and there were a few crumbling stalls. I looked up. There was more sky than roof. It was a miserable place.

'See what they did?' complained the farmer. 'They made a fire, damn 'em, and could 'ave burned down my best barn! The embers were still warm the next morning.'

Indeed, we could see the remains of a fire in the middle of the floor. But the barn had been perfectly safe, for the thieves had banked up the fire with earth so that the straw around would not catch. It looked as though several men had been here. There were horse droppings scattered about and different-sized footprints in the dust and dirt.

'Search the place thoroughly, gentlemen,' ordered Mr Hatton. 'The men may still be here, or have left something that gives us another clue to their identities. Where did you find the gun, man?'

The farmer pointed to the corner of one of the empty stalls. Mr Hatton went to inspect it while his guards drew their swords and began to poke and prod about the farmyard. Mary and I stayed with the farmer, who stood with his feet nearly in the ashes of the fire. But we didn't stand too close, for the smell was appalling!

'My poor old Bessie and Annie and Kitty,' muttered the farmer. 'Where be my little biddies now? In some fox's belly, I'll be bound.

Wicked, wicked varmints to do this to a poor old man. If I ever get 'old of 'em they'll wish the Devil 'imself and all 'is 'ellhounds had caught 'em instead.'

At last the Gentlemen of the Guard had finished their search. They had found nothing, so Mr Hatton called us all to our horses.

'The thieves are long gone,' he said. 'There is nothing more we can learn here. But you did well, sir.' He tossed a coin to the farmer.

The old man was certainly keen to have it, for there was no fumbling in his catch. He bit the coin in his dirty yellow teeth and bowed to Mr Hatton. 'All in a day's work, yer honour,' he grunted.

As we rode back to Windsor, I felt uneasy. Several things about the mystery did not add up. It seemed certain that men and horses had stayed in the barn at the pig farm, and the ivory-handled pistol was found in one of the stalls. But I was struck by the fact that Seth and the Gentlemen of the Guard had only ever mentioned seeing *one* thief. So was there one felon or three? And were any of the thieves also courtiers, or were they just sturdy beggars, as Mr Hatton believes? Certainly the evidence from the pig farm seemed to confirm the drunkard's words, and suggested that Mr Hatton was right. But I could not shake the feeling that at least one of the thieves was a gentleman. By all accounts he had behaved like a gentleman during the robbery, and Seth had remarked that he had a fine horse. Besides, something about the pig farm itself bothered me – and troubles me still – though I cannot put my finger on just what it is. My instincts tell me that my investigation should not end just yet.

We arrived back at the castle and rode into the Tilting Yard, where our horses were taken from us. I glanced at the sundial as we made for the Queen's Apartments. It was nearly one of the clock and I still had not eaten. The only path I wished to take was the one that led to the Great Kitchen, but I knew I could not. I had to hear what Mr Hatton was going to tell the Queen.

Her Majesty was with Mr Secretary Cecil

in her Privy Chamber. She was already dressed for the wedding, and looked resplendent. She had probably started at dawn. It is a mixed blessing to have Her Majesty at a wedding, for a bride will always be outshone by her. Her gown was of black and white striped silk with gold lace. She wore a heavy collar of pearls and rubies with matching armlets, and on her breast was pinned a brooch of gold, which had tiny rubies and emeralds surrounding a black agate stone. She had been given it by Queen Catherine Howard when she was only seven. It may be thought old-fashioned but I knew the Queen was very fond of it.

There were State papers piled on one of the tables and I could see the remains of her noontide meal at another. Mr Hatton did not question my presence as I followed him in. In truth he did not realize I was behind him, and gave a start of surprise as I suddenly appeared at his side with my basket of asparagus.

'Well, Mr Hatton,' said Her Majesty. 'What news?'

'My Liege,' answered Mr Hatton, giving me

a sideways look, 'my report is privy and I would not—'

'Get on with it, man!' snapped the Queen impatiently.

Mr Hatton looked as if he would like to shake off his unwanted follower but he did as the Queen bade him. 'Your Majesty,' he said gravely, 'my suspicions are confirmed. It was indeed a band of brigands who made off with your loan. They evaded my men in the forest but did not travel far. It is likely they wished to throw us off their scent, for there were signs that they spent the rest of the night of the robbery at a pig farm hard by the village.'

'Then do you believe that they are still close to Meadowfold?' asked the Queen.

'I do, Your Majesty.' Mr Hatton nodded. 'I think the felons may be within our grasp, and to that end I shall dispatch a goodly number of my guards to scour the forest. Have no fear, My Liege. If they are there they shall be caught.'

'I doubt it not, good sir,' said Her Majesty. 'I trust you to attend to the matter without delay.'

Mr Hatton bowed his way out. I noticed that he shut the doors to the chamber somewhat hastily – perhaps he thought I would try to follow him again!

As soon as he had gone, Her Majesty turned to me. 'You look pale, Grace,' she said, with a note of concern in her voice. 'Was the ride too arduous for you? Or is it disappointment that your . . . mission is at an end?'

'It is neither, Your Majesty,' I said faintly. 'It is merely that I am famished. I have not broken my fast today.'

'Then we must remedy that,' laughed the Queen, and she ordered me to sit and finish the remnants of her meal. Fortunately the kitchen always sends Her Majesty a good selection of platters and she eats sparingly, so there was plenty for me. Mr Secretary Cecil went back to his papers, but the Queen came to my side.

'I am glad that you can cease your investigations, my Lady Pursuivant,' she said in a low voice, 'for it troubles me that you are sometimes near to danger in your duty to the Crown. Now you can be content that the theft is the work of sturdy beggars and not someone at Court.' She turned and called to Sir William Cecil. 'Make ready the French papers, Mr Secretary.'

As far as the Queen was concerned the matter was closed. She would not have listened to my doubts, so I sat and ate my way through two pigeon pasties, a huge hunk of cheese and three sugared apricots. All the while my thoughts were tumbling over and over in my head. If the thief, or one of the thieves, was at Court, who could it possibly be? And what was it about the pig farm that so disturbed me? A glimmer of something began to stir in my brain when the Queen suddenly rose.

'It is well past one of the clock, Grace dear,' she reminded me. 'You must bestir yourself else you will be late for the marriage ceremony.'

Faith! The wedding! I thought and with many a hurried curtsy I left the Queen's presence and fled for my chamber. I knew I needed to write down all the morning's events and leave myself time to dress! But I had only just left the Queen's Apartments when I heard a *Pssst!* from behind a closet door. I looked over to see Masou and Ellie beckoning to me. My time was very short but I could not leave my friends in suspense. I made sure I was unobserved and joined them: there was not much space in the small room, for it was full of chairs and folded card tables.

'How did you fare, Grace?' whispered Ellie excitedly.

I told them all about my ride to Meadowfold.

'So Her Majesty's Lady Pursuivant is in a quandary,' said Masou. 'Here is a puzzle indeed. We have a long journey completed in but a short time. We have expert riders who cannot keep in their saddles. And we have one man who turns into three.' His black eyes twinkled. 'Surely there is magic afoot!'

'Hush, Masou!' I laughed. 'Ellie is going pale with fear!'

''Taint fear!' snorted Ellie. 'I was thinking about the pig farm. I'm glad now I didn't go with you. I hate the smell of pigs!'

'I confess I did not notice the smell,' I said, 'for the farmer himself reeked enough for twenty swine! But something does not sit right with me about that place. And I would still swear that one of the thieves is a gentleman.'

'You may have to admit you are wrong this time, my Lady Grace,' teased Masou, tweaking the feather in my hat, 'for 'twould seem that the esteemed Mr Hatton has the right of it and the gold was stolen by bandits.'

'Then I hope his guards find them soon,' declared Ellie stoutly. 'For anyone who steals from our dear Queen deserves to be caught and shot – with his own pistol!'

I gave her a hug. 'You are a loyal subject, Ellie,' I said. 'And I have not given up my investigation just yet. Now I must away. I wish to write all this down in my daybooke and get dressed for the wedding!'

I have just looked down into the Tilting Yard and there are people beginning to bustle about! I must make haste to my bedchamber, stow my daybooke and hope that Mrs Champernowne has not missed me.

Fiddlesticks! I have just remembered I left the asparagus in the Queen's Privy Chamber. I hope someone has taken it to the kitchen.

Late, in my bedchamber

It is late and Lady Sarah is at last asleep. She has been in a dreadful temper. I found it very irksome, for I needed peace to write in my daybooke. Even when we were in our beds she would not desist – despite Mary Shelton's attempts to pacify her.

'I cannot credit the behaviour of certain gentlemen of the Court,' seethed Lady Sarah, gripping her bedcovers as if she would rip them to pieces.

'Do not think on these matters now,' said Mary Shelton soothingly.

'How can I not think on them?' Lady Sarah exploded. 'Sir Roger Spratling gave me to believe he would promise me marriage on this very day. Mrs Champernowne said it is a good omen to become betrothed on the day of another's wedding. Yet he has kept his silence!'

'Oh, Lady Sarah,' said Mary, leaning over and patting her arm. 'I am so sorry. I did not realize that you truly wished to marry Sir Roger.'

'In truth I did not,' Lady Sarah retorted, 'but I did expect to be asked!'

'Sir Roger may still ask you. There are other days—' began Mary.

'Fie on other days!' exclaimed Sarah. 'He will have no other days with me. I have discovered that he did not even purchase the necklace he gave me. It was just some unwanted trinket of his mother's! If he believes I would marry such a miser he must needs think again.' She hugged the bedclothes around her. 'I shall keep the necklace though,' she added firmly. 'It looks well with my blue silk partlet and sleeves.' Then she remembered how cross she was. 'But I am sure I shall not sleep a wink tonight for sorrow.'

I give thanks to the Lord that she has not kept her word and is now snoring soundly, for I have much of importance to write. This mystery has taken another new twist! And it was actually Penelope's wedding that revealed the most shocking clue.

As soon as I had spotted the crowds gathering in the Tilting Yard, ready for the wedding, I dashed back down to my bedchamber to stow my daybooke under my pillow. Mrs Champernowne must have finished her improving readings, for Mary Shelton and Lady Sarah were back.

Mary was helping Sarah adjust her hat. 'Mrs Champernowne has been looking for you, Grace,' she said. 'I tried to keep her at bay but you know how persistent she is. Where have you been?'

And indeed, at that moment Mrs Champernowne herself sailed in. She was red in the face and clutching a basket of dried rose petals. She stopped short at the sight of me. I tried to look as if I had been sitting there waiting for her. But in vain.

'Have you taken leave of your senses, Grace?' she demanded, sounding more Welsh than usual in her bad temper. 'There is a wedding at any moment, look you. Her Majesty is ready to proceed to the chapel and you have been off enjoying yourself, I'll warrant. All the other Maids have been listening to *Pious Thoughts on Holy Matrimony* and you would have done well to join us!' She studied my gown. 'Well!' she sniffed. 'A black apron at a wedding? Take it off at once before you bring ill omens upon us all!' I struggled with the knot at the back while she poked her head out into the passage. 'Fran!' she called. 'Bring the tussie-mussies. We are all here at last!'

Fran hurried forwards with the little posies tied with ribbons. They were made mostly of herbs and smelled sweet. Peeking through the sage and marjoram were tiny forget-me-nots. (I have mine still and have laid it in my chest amongst my petticoats.)

Clutching our tussie-mussies, we joined Carmina and Lady Jane and made our way to the Presence Chamber. The Queen shone and everyone was complimenting her on her magnificent gown. There was no doubt that eyes would go to her sooner than to Penelope

– and that is how she likes it. She took the arm of Sir William Cecil and led the bridal party down the grand staircase and out across the Engine Court. I followed with the other Maids.

Here we met Penelope and her father. Penelope looked radiant. She was attired in a rich red silk gown in the Spanish style. The skirts were cut to show the forepart, which was a darker red with a raised looped pile in silver metal thread. She wore slashed sleeves, the slashes brought together with silver aiglets, and there were tiny pearls stitched into the ruffs. The pearls were a wedding gift from Her Majesty. In the old custom Penelope carried a garland of rosemary and roses. (Of course, the roses were dried because of the season.) Red ribbons tied in love knots dangled from the garland. Penelope wore no hat, for she would have the garland placed on her head when she came out of the chapel as Thomas's wife.

We walked down to the chapel, holding Her Majesty's train in our customary fashion as

Maids of Honour, with Mrs Champernowne behind us. It felt strange not having Penelope beside us. She was following with her father, Sir John Knollys, who would be giving her away. Her mother, sisters and old Lady Knollys were behind them.

Mrs Champernowne was muttering under her breath about wedding superstitions. 'Now, the sun is shining,' she murmured. 'That is a good omen. And there should be no nuns or monks to cast barrenness and poverty on Penelope and Thomas, but the sight of a lamb or a toad would not come amiss . . .'

The Gentlemen of the Guard lined our path from the Upper to the Lower Ward of the castle. They stood smartly to attention as the harbingers in their red tabards played a fanfare to greet Her Majesty's arrival. The April sun sparkled on their trumpets. It was a fine sight.

Then I noticed a young kitchen lad hiding behind Samuel Twyer, who was standing in the line of guards. The boy had a squirming black cat in his arms. As we drew closer, Mrs Champernowne waved frantically at him and he loosed the cat, which tried to run away from the wedding party and had to be chivvied across in front of us by a sly nudge from the boy.

'There's luck, Penelope!' called Mrs Champernowne, as if it was a surprise to her. 'To have a black cat run across your path.'

I am sure I heard the Queen chuckle. And it was truly kind of Mrs Champernowne to arrange such good fortune for the happy couple.

We were a noisy crowd. The harbingers had ceased their fanfare, but now the Court musicians joined the procession, playing pipes and tabors. However, most of the clamour came from Thomas's friends, who jostled along with the rest of the Court and had probably partaken of more mead than usual. Thomas walked slightly apart with Lord Ruxbury, his best man. Thomas looked nervous. Mayhap he was scared of the Queen. He knew how disappointed she was to be losing one of her Maids of Honour.

'This is so exciting,' I heard Carmina

whisper to Mary Shelton. 'Yet I shall miss Penelope sorely.'

Suddenly Sir John Knollys gave a cry. I turned to see him sitting on the cobbles. I confess I wanted to laugh at the sight of Mrs Champernowne trying to pull him to his feet and clucking about ill omens all the while.

'This is because you are marrying after noon has struck,' she scolded Penelope, as she flapped about the poor man. 'There's bad luck, look you.'

'Mrs Champernowne!' exclaimed Her Majesty sternly. 'I would remind you that I fixed on the time of four of the clock as the most convenient to all parties. The only ill fortune here is an errant cobble that has twisted Sir John's ankle. Now, attend to his needs.' Then her expression softened. 'And do not forget,' she said, 'the month is most auspicious and will counter any bad luck, for is it not said, "Marry in April when you can, joy for the maiden and the man?"'

Poor Sir John was finding it difficult to bear weight on his ankle and needed to lean heavily on one of the guards while Mrs Champernowne fussed around offering to fetch poultices and bandages. Penelope looked as if she were going to cry, but then Lord Ruxbury stepped forward and offered her his arm.

'It would be the greatest of honours,' he said gallantly, 'if you would allow me to escort you to the chapel.'

He is such a gentleman! And he brought the smile back to Penelope's face.

We processed in through the Galilee Porch at the east of the chapel. It is very old – about three hundred years, I have heard. I used to enjoy tracing the curling wrought ironwork of its door with my fingers – but only when I was very little, of course.

There was not enough room in the choir for us all to stand at the altar, so many of the Court filed around to the main chapel. They would be able to hear the service, for Canon Edmund Freke has a loud voice.

The Maids of Honour had a good view from the steps next to the Queen's stall. It seemed that old Lady Knollys was not as lucky. She was standing behind portly Sir Pelham Poucher. 'Forsooth,' she boomed, 'I cannot see anything of my Penelope! Never have I beheld such a big stout body!' Thankfully, Sir Pelham is rather deaf.

Her Majesty motioned to Canon Freke to proceed. Penelope and Thomas stood together in front of the altar. The sun was filtering through the stained glass and it was as if Heaven itself were smiling on them. (Faith, I am becoming a poet! Look out, Mr Naunton!)

Lord Ruxbury stood by Thomas's right side. This is an old tradition. I believe it was Lord Ruxbury's duty to protect Thomas's sword arm in case anyone tried to steal his bride away! I did not think anyone was going to today, however.

'Dearly beloved,' intoned Canon Freke, 'we are gathered together here in the sight of God to join together this man and this woman in holy matrimony.'

At these words, Penelope's mother began to sniff into a kerchief.

'Calm yourself, Letitia,' bellowed old Lady Knollys, making everyone jump. 'You will disturb the ceremony!'

The words of the marriage service are beautiful, I am sure, but Canon Freke has a sonorous voice and speaks very slowly. I confess my attention began to wander back to the mystery. I was no nearer to defining that nagging unease about the pig farm, yet it seemed to call to me with urgency. What could it be? It was all so perplexing. I had no answers and I started to fear I might not be able to serve Her Majesty in this matter after all.

But I was wool-gathering and that would never do. Thomas was making his vows. He gazed into Penelope's eyes as the priest asked him if he would take her to be his lawful wedded wife and look after her for ever. Well, there was a lot more to it than that but I have not the time to put it all down.

'I will,' said Thomas in a loud voice.

Now the Canon turned to Penelope with the same question.

'I will,' she whispered.

The Canon nodded and smiled.

'Who giveth this woman to be married to this man?' he asked.

Sir John Knollys limped painfully forwards, leaning heavily on the arm of his son.

'I do,' he answered proudly. He took Penelope's right hand and placed it in Canon Freke's. Then he shuffled back.

The canon took Thomas's right hand and placed it over Penelope's. Then they plighted their troth, which just means they promised not to fall in love with anyone else. It does seem to take a long time to get yourself wed!

Lord Ruxbury now stepped forwards and handed a ring to the Canon. (I wonder what would have happened if he had lost the ring! Could they still be wed?) Then came my favourite part of the wedding ceremony. Canon Freke blessed the ring and gave it to Thomas, who placed it upon Penelope's thumb.

'With this ring I thee wed,' he said. Then he put the ring on her index finger. 'With my body I thee honour, and with all my worldly goods I thee endow.' And with that he took the gold band and set it upon her ring finger. I do not know why the middle finger is missed out, but that is how it is always done.

Penelope will not take the ring off to show us, but she has told us that it is inscribed with these words:

I AM YOURS, LOVE ME TRULY

AFTER CONSENT, EVER CONTENT

LOVE ME AND LEAVE ME NOT

Verily that is a lot of words for such a small ring!

With the vows all said, we processed out through the Galilee Porch again. Mrs Champernowne showered the couple with her dried rose petals, some of Thomas's friends pelted them with shoes for luck, and the atmosphere was very merry indeed.

We all went to St George's Hall for the wedding revels. I entered just behind Lord Ruxbury. I wished to tell him how kind I thought he had been to escort Penelope – well, really I wanted to hear his imitation of Canon

Freke – but before I could speak to him he fell into conversation with the Earl of Leicester, so I had to bide my time. But I made sure I stood close so that I could gain his attention when he was free.

'That was a most excellent hunt yesterday, my lord,' Lord Ruxbury said. 'You keep a fine stock of harts here at Windsor.'

'I thank you, sir,' answered the Earl of Leicester with a bow. 'What think you of the dogs? I warrant you have never seen better.'

'No, indeed,' agreed Lord Ruxbury. 'They forced the deer to run as if the Devil himself and all his Hellhounds were after them.'

I was struck by his turn of phrase, for I had heard that expression before, and only this morning. The pig farmer had used it when describing the felons. And so had the drunkard at the crossroads! How curious that Lord Ruxbury should use the very same words. Then I thought of his wonderful imitations and I felt my mind spin as an utterly incredible idea hit me. Could it be that the drunkard and the pig farmer were one and the same person – Lord Ruxbury in disguise?

The more I thought about it, the more I realized that the pig farmer at least could indeed have been Lord Ruxbury. Mary and I were so busy avoiding the dreadful smell emanating from the man that we deliberately did not stare at his face, for fear he would feel encouraged to step closer and speak to us. Thus I had not recognized the pig farmer as Lord Ruxbury, even though he spoke directly to me! What a brilliantly clever disguise!

Indeed, if Lord Ruxbury was the thief, what a clever crime he had committed altogether – and how cool-headed he had been. After all, he must have carried out the robbery, then sat boldly by the road, playing the drunkard, to set a false trail for Mr Hatton's men. Then this morning he returned in the guise of a pig farmer to lead us all to a deserted farm and convince us that the real thieves were sturdy beggars who had made off into the forest. And at last I realized what had so bothered me about the pig farm: there had not been a pig in sight!

I have to admit that although wrong had been done to the Queen, the sheer daring of the crime quickened my pulse!

But suddenly I realized I was allowing my imagination to run wild, for I had forgotten about the timing of the robbery. A man would need a very fast horse if he was going to leave Court at near two in the morning and be back at just after five – the time that Lord Ruxbury was seen in the kitchen. Minstrel was indeed fast and Lord Ruxbury had the skill to ride her on such a mission, but all the witnesses had agreed that the thief's horse was completely black, while Minstrel's white markings are very distinctive. And surely Lord Ruxbury does not have another horse that could get him to Meadowfold and back in barely three and a half hours.

I knew I must be careful not to make accusations until I had evidence. Lord Ruxbury might have had nothing to do with the crime at all. It could be mere coincidence that he had used the same words as the drunkard and the pig farmer. I was determined to prove his innocence – or his guilt.

I decided to start by trying to find the gold and jewels. If Lord Ruxbury was the thief they might still be in the saddlebags that Hugh Morling had been forced to pack. But where were those saddlebags now? In the stables? Or taken from there and hidden in his bedchamber?

While Lord Ruxbury was occupied with the celebrations I had the perfect chance to have both those places searched. Of course, a Maid of Honour could not be seen in a gentleman's bedchamber, but a laundrymaid could! Ellie would arouse no suspicion if she were found there with an armful of linen.

But I had no easy way of leaving the celebrations to speak to Ellie myself. I would have to send a trusted messenger, and there was only one person who could fill those shoes: Masou. I knew I should waste no time in finding him. But fortune was against me: at that moment a great fanfare sounded and the crowds parted to leave a space in the middle of the hall. The Queen, Penelope and Thomas had seats while the rest of us stood. Mr Somers's troupe burst in, arrayed in their brightest garb and led by Masou. They each carried a bow and arrow and stopped to strike a pose like statues of Eros, God of Love.

Mr Somers came forwards and bowed deeply to the Queen. 'Your Majesty,' he announced. 'On this most joyous of days we humbly beg your indulgence as we show you our skills . . .'

Mr Somers's speeches can be very witty, with many a pun, but today I could not listen to the rest of it. I wished it to be at an end, for every second counted. Then Lord Ruxbury caught my eye and smiled. My stomach flipped over. I suddenly realized that if he was the villain, I did not want to be the one to find him out. He has shown me nothing but kindness and friendship. He bowed most graciously, so I tried to nod politely back and prayed he did not see the confusion on my face. I turned and watched the troupe with what I hope looked like rapt attention.

It was easy to feign interest, for the troupe performed magnificently. The 'statues' threw down their bows and arrows and began a frenzy of rapid somersaults and jumps. At times I thought they would collide with each other but their timing was perfect and there was many an *Ooh* and *Ah* from the assembled courtiers. Masou certainly could not help me at the moment.

I began to wonder if I could somehow slip out myself to find Ellie, or if I could pretend a faint and be taken to my bedchamber. But I decided against the latter, for it would cause a commotion and I wanted to avoid that. I concluded I would have to wait until the entertainment had finished: it was just too difficult for me to escape unnoticed.

Now the tumblers were gathered round a scene in the centre of the floor. I realized that they were depicting the old Greek story of the return of Odysseus to his faithful wife, Penelope. There sat Masou as Penelope, in long robes and a black wig, weaving sadly at a loom and waiting for her husband to return to her after twenty long years. She had her old dog at her side. (This was Gypsy Pete, the youngest member of the troupe, dressed in furs with floppy ears and a long droopy tail.) Masou did not look as if he knew how to weave at all! Luckily for him he was saved from a woolly entanglement by the arrival of French Louis as Odysseus. He strode in, swathed in white, to claim his wife from all the false suitors who were on their knees, pleading with her to marry them. Everyone seemed to have forgotten that although Penelope was always a faithful wife, the Odysseus of Greek myth had many adventures with other fair ladies before he came home to her!

But whatever the truth behind it, the scene depicting her namesake obviously delighted our Penelope. Gypsy Pete made a great show of being the elderly dog who, according to the legend, saw his master and died forthwith. He flopped around, wiggling his bottom like a puppy, then keeled over and lay as if dead.

The Court was delighted by the display and there was a great burst of applause. (All the while, Gypsy Pete lay with his legs stiffly in the air and finally had to be carried off by Mr

Somers.) As soon as Masou had gone I made my way to the doors the troupe had used for their exit. Preparations for the feast were underway and I was able to slip out for a moment without being spotted.

Masou was just taking off his wig and scratching his head when he saw me. 'My lady,' he exclaimed, sweeping a great bow with the wig in his hand like a hat. 'I trust our humble performance was pleasing to your ladyship, for it is our greatest joy to—'

'Do not play the fool now, Masou!' I hissed. 'I have need of you.'

Masou winked. 'Mr Somers,' he called to his master. 'I beg to withdraw. Lady Grace Cavendish has come with some most helpful censure of my acting and I would hear it privately.'

'Perhaps my lady could instruct poor Penelope in the gentle art of the loom!' said Mr Somers, grinning, and still carrying Gypsy Pete in his arms. 'As for me, I have to attend to this dead dog. I must needs bury it directly before it starts to stink!' With that Gypsy Pete jumped down with a squeal and scuttled away.

Masou laughed. 'Gypsy Pete took his role most seriously!' he said. 'Unlike Mr Somers's puppy Castor, who could not be used as he would do nothing but lick my fingers and bite the weaving wool!'

I pulled Masou aside to an alcove where no one would hear us.

He looked hard at me. 'What is the matter?' he asked.

'I have a new suspect!' I whispered urgently. 'But no proof of his felony and therefore—'

'Therefore,' Masou grinned, 'having not the brains to do it yourself, you need my cunning to find the clues. Is it not so?'

'No, it is not, you want-wit!' I exclaimed impatiently. 'In truth it is Ellie I need. Would you find her and give her a message from me?'

Masou rolled his eyes. 'So humble a task for one so gifted!' he sighed, shaking his head sadly. 'Pray tell me, what on this fair earth can Ellie do that I cannot?'

I quickly explained my plan. Then I had a sudden thought. 'And be sure to tell her,' I added, 'that if the gold is not there she is to search for other signs of felony.'

When I had finished his eyes lit up. 'Then she will need a lookout,' he said, 'and that will be my role.'

With that he pulled up his robes and skipped away like a young girl. Masou had the right of it: Ellie could be in some danger if she was discovered rummaging in chests and boxes where there was no dirty laundry.

Meanwhile I made straight for Her Majesty. I was desperate to waste no more time. I was determined to convince her of the urgency of my mission.

I approached and knelt before her. 'Your Majesty,' I said, holding my hand to my temples as if in pain. 'I have something pounding in my head and beg your leave to retire for a little until it has gone.'

'A trifling headache, and you demand to leave my presence, Grace?' said the Queen sharply. 'I had thought you made of sterner stuff than this.'

'I would not for all Your Majesty's *gold*

displease My Liege,' I said carefully, hoping she would catch my meaning. 'With luck I may root out the cause of this pain, for I have a notion as to where it is lodged.'

I saw the Queen's dark brown eyes give the faintest of flickers. She looked piercingly at me. 'Are you certain that this . . . ache is not imagined, Grace?' she demanded.

'I am most sure, Your Majesty,' I answered. I have had coded speech with Her Majesty before. I am always thankful that she has such a quick mind, and so nothing of our true meaning is gleaned by anyone else who listens.

'Then go, child,' said the Queen, feigning irritation. 'But be not long or you will know my anger. Take Mary Shelton with you! And take care . . . of your head.'

As the stables are outside the walls of the castle I needed to take a companion with me. Beshrew these rules where ladies of the Court may not venture out alone! If I were Queen I should pass a decree that they are perfectly safe on their own, if they keep their wits sharp. I told Mary Shelton that I needed to visit the stables and that the Queen wanted her to accompany me. It was most urgent that I talk to Perkin there as I feared my mare was lame. Mary agreed at once but told me she would not come into the stable itself as she hates to see a horse in distress. Instead she would take herself to Perkin's cousin's wife, who lives in one of the cottages by the stables and has just given birth. Mary truly does know everyone!

We passed through the Castle Gate and made quickly for the stables, where Mary left me. As soon as I entered the stable block I went to find Perkin. Perkin loves the horses in his care. He even sleeps among them. Soon I heard a familiar whistling from the other end of the building and Perkin came out of one of the stables.

He stopped in surprise at the sight of me. 'Lady Grace!' he bowed, pulling at his cap. 'What brings you to the stable when I hear there is a marriage today?' He grinned. 'Perhaps you are like me and would sooner spend your time with these fine and well-mannered beasts than with some of yonder Court! But forgive me, my lady. I spoke too freely!'

I could not tell Perkin that I agreed with him so I smiled instead to show he had not angered me. I began to wonder how to work round to the real purpose of my visit!

'I fear that Doucette may have shown some signs of lameness this morning,' I told him, feeling rather flustered at giving such a feeble reason to leave a wedding feast! 'I meant to tell you when we returned from our journey, but I only remembered just now.'

'Let us go and check, my lady,' said Perkin, looking worried. 'Although I shall think myself a noddlehead if there is aught amiss. For I pride myself in looking after the horses in my care as if they were my own.'

'I have no doubt of it,' I assured him, as we made for my mare's stable. I felt sorry. I had not meant Perkin, my favourite stable lad, to think that he had made a mistake.

Doucette certainly showed no signs of lameness when Perkin walked her up and down.

'She is perfectly sound,' I said. 'I apologize, Perkin, for it seems that *I* am the noddlehead!'

'Never, my lady!' exclaimed Perkin, turning as pink as if he had called me a noddlehead himself.

'But you can help me further,' I went on quickly. 'I have been thinking of buying some new saddlebags. Lord Ruxbury tells me that his are fashioned of the finest leather this side of the Alps. May I see them?'

Perkin was only too eager to oblige and led me to Minstrel's stable.

Minstrel looked sleek and glossy with her majestic white blaze. She nuzzled me with her nose.

'That's strange,' said Perkin, scratching his head as he looked around. 'The saddlebags should be hanging right here. By your leave I will go and look for them.' He hurried off, and I wondered if this might mean Ellie would have luck finding them in Lord Ruxbury's chamber.

I stroked Minstrel's silky neck. She shifted her feet to move nearer and I heard a strange chink. She had kicked against something in her stable. It sounded metallic. There should only be straw about her hooves, so I wondered what it could be.

Nudging Minstrel gently to one side, I entered the stall and felt about in the hay while keeping a wary eye on her feet. She is a trustworthy mare, but I feared she would not know what I was about and might think that I meant her harm. I soon found the source of the noise. It was a tin casket. I picked it up and opened it to find it was full of soot! What in Heaven's name was this doing in Minstrel's stable? I asked myself. Had one of the stable lads accidentally left it lying in the straw? I dabbed my finger in and looked at the black mark on my skin.

And suddenly I realized that this was no stable lad's casket. Gently I stroked a tiny bit of the soot onto the white blaze on Minstrel's nose. The hair turned black where I touched. Now I knew without a doubt that Lord Ruxbury was the thief and that Minstrel had carried him to Meadowfold and back. He had turned his mare into a pure black horse by rubbing soot onto her white blaze and socks! He truly was a bold adventurer to make such a journey and take on the Gentlemen of the Guard, I thought. And he had covered his tracks well. If I had not overheard that chance remark – '. . . as if the Devil himself and all his Hellhounds were after them' – that Lord Ruxbury made to the Earl of Leicester, I would never have suspected him. I could not help being impressed by Lord Ruxbury's cleverness and skill – and yet I must bring him to justice if I can. My first loyalty is to the Queen.

I heard footsteps and quickly hid the casket under the straw and brushed the soot from Minstrel's nose. Suppose it was Lord Ruxbury, how would I explain what I was doing here? To my great relief, it was Perkin's face that appeared over the stable door. He looked most anxious.

'I have searched the stables from top to bottom,' he said, 'and I can find neither hide nor hair of Lord Ruxbury's saddlebags!'

'Oh, Perkin!' I declared. 'I am indeed a noddlehead, for did not his lordship himself tell me he would take his bags to show the Earl of Leicester? I believe the Earl was as interested as I to see the fine leather. You are not to worry.'

'I am glad of it,' sighed Perkin, wiping his brow. 'For I would not want to do wrong by that kind gentleman.'

Lord Ruxbury is indeed a well-liked nobleman! I stroked Minstrel again. 'This is a magnificent mare, is she not?' I said, hoping to engage him in some further speech.

'She's a rare 'un,' Perkin replied eagerly. 'Never a bite nor a kick from this beauty. And that Lord Ruxbury is a rare owner. He treats her like royalty. He even insists on mucking out her stable himself. 'Tis unheard of for a lord to do such a thing – but he does it, upon my soul.'

So that explained why the soot had not been discovered.

'He is not like some of them,' snorted Perkin. 'Some care little for their horses, although I say it as shouldn't. A number of them went out galloping early this morning.

It were Mr Penn and his friends — off to use up some energy before the wedding, I'll be bound. Yet it were only Lord Ruxbury who attended his horse after. He was later than them and they joked that he'd got himself lost and Mr Penn offered me the post of best man if he didn't come back!'

So I now knew that Lord Ruxbury had gone out on Minstrel this morning. But what about the night of the robbery?

'You may be needed yet as best man, Perkin,' I giggled. 'I hear talk of another wedding, for three nights since, on the night of the twentieth, Sir Roger Spratling rode all the way to London to fetch his love a gift. Did you saddle his horse for him?' In fact, I knew it had been the night of the twenty-first that Sir Roger had gone to get Lady Sarah's necklace, but I was keen to get Perkin talking about the night of the robbery.

There was no fooling Perkin, however. He frowned. 'Indeed, I believe it was the night of the twenty-first that Sir Roger rode to London, my lady,' he said. 'For the night of the twentieth – 'twas the night of the robbery, and no one rode out then.'

'How can you be sure?' I exclaimed.

'I remember that night well,' said Perkin with a grin. ''Twas that day my cousin was blessed with a fine baby boy, and Lord Ruxbury, who is an open-handed gentleman, brought me a flagon of ale to wet the baby's head. I slept most soundly that night!'

'Then you may not have heard anyone come to the stable,' I insisted.

'If it had been Sir Roger Spratling,' Perkin declared, 'I'd have felt his boot in my ribs as I did the night he went to London! He might have his own groom, but he'd not stand by and let me sleep.'

But Lord Ruxbury would have, I thought to myself. And Lord Ruxbury would also have made certain that Perkin heard nothing. I wondered whether there had been an extra ingredient in that ale to make Perkin sleep so soundly.

I had learned enough, and so I went to find Mary Shelton. After I had admired the new baby's eyes (like his mother's) and his nose (like his father's) we made our way back to the festivities. My mind was in a ferment. Although I was certain that I knew at last who the thief was, it would be no simple matter to convince Her Majesty – and Mr Hatton – of Lord Ruxbury's guilt without evidence. I prayed that Ellie had found the Queen's gold and jewels in his bedchamber. And then almost at once I hoped she had not. In the past I have found out villains who meant Her Majesty ill and rejoiced at it, but I do not believe Lord Ruxbury is a cold-hearted miscreant; he has shown too much kindness. It is so confusing. My heart says one thing and my head another.

My head won. I had to carry on. I needed to see Ellie and Masou. And as if I had conjured them up with my thoughts, I saw my two friends lurking round the side of the Banqueting Hall. I thanked Mary for her company, made my excuses and went to join them.

'Did you find the gold?' I asked eagerly.

'I searched every nook and cranny, God

forgive me,' said Ellie. 'But I found no gold, nor no jewels neither.'

'But Ellie did discover something of note,' added Masou.

'Indeed I did,' said Ellie proudly. 'A little jar at the very bottom of his clothes press. I opened it and we had a sniff—'

'And it contained syrup of poppy,' finished Masou. 'I wonder whom Lord Ruxbury might send to the land of dreams with that!'

'Perkin the stableboy!' I exclaimed. Their eyes grew wide as I told them what I had learned.

'Then Lord Ruxbury is truly the thief,' said Masou. 'And a bold one at that, to have made such a ride and stolen the Queen's gold! But still we lack the treasure! Where can it be hidden? Ask it of us, my lady, and Ellie and I will take the castle apart with our bare hands looking for it, stone by stone!'

'Don't be a clod, Masou!' laughed Ellie. 'Her Majesty would have something to say if she saw her castle down about her ankles.' She scratched her chin. 'Surely someone would have seen him lugging them saddlebags about instead of leaving them in the stable like everyone else? They'd be very heavy with all that gold. Shall we ask among the servants?'

I clapped my hand to my brow. 'I have been a featherbrain!' I declared, to their surprise. 'We know that Lord Ruxbury must have ridden like the wind, for one of the guards heard the church clock strike half after three as the thief escaped Meadowfold, and the Head Cook in the Great Kitchen saw him back in Windsor shortly after five. Well, he most certainly could not have travelled so swiftly with saddlebags of gold and jewels weighing him down. I warrant he did not bring them back with him at all!'

Ellie snorted in disbelief. 'So what did he do then?' she asked. 'Give the gold to the poor? He's no Robin Hood, I'll be bound.'

'No indeed!' I exclaimed. 'I think he hid it at Meadowfold!'

'But what of his accomplices, Grace?' asked Masou. 'Would he not have handed the gold to them?'

This gave me pause, but then I remembered when Lord Ruxbury and I had danced together. We had talked of the thieves. And now I could hear his very words ringing in my head: '. . . if it were just one man,' he had told me, 'he could have all the treasure to himself. A lone thief would be a happy thief indeed.'

'I am certain there were no accomplices,' I told Masou. 'The only witnesses who say there was more than one thief were the pig farmer and the drunkard – and, as we know, they were both Lord Ruxbury.' Then I gasped. 'I think I know where the gold is! Indeed, Lord Ruxbury took us right to the place – how like him to be so daring.'

'The pig farm?' queried Masou. 'Yet it was searched, was it not? He must have hidden his booty very cleverly.'

'What a bold villain!' exclaimed Ellie in wonder.

'Yet I cannot help but admire his cunning,' I remarked. 'Even while disapproving of his actions, of course,' I added quickly. 'Ellie, I must needs ride to the pig farm outside Meadowfold at dawn tomorrow and—'

'You wish me to wake you again,' sighed Ellie.

'Indeed I do,' I agreed. 'But more than that. I wish you and Masou to come with me. We are going to find the gold!'

A few moments later

I had to attend to my candle as it was spluttering fit to die and I still have more to write. With luck it will last a while longer.

Once Ellie had stopped shrieking with delight at the thought of the adventure, I asked her if she would get into trouble for being absent all morning. Ellie paused for a moment to think about this, but then her eyes lit up. She had remembered that Mrs Fadget was to be busy all the morning on some errands for Mrs Twiste, and Ellie was confident that nobody else would quiz her on her absence.

So we quickly made our plans, for I soon had to return to the festivities.

'We shall ride to Meadowfold on the morrow and begin our search!' I declared.

'Hold, Grace!' laughed Masou, raising his hands. 'You have forgotten two things. Ellie and I have no mounts!'

'That is but one thing!' I protested.

'No, fair Grace.' Masou grinned. 'For do we not need a mount each? Your arithmetic is poor indeed if you do not know that one and one makes two!'

I did not answer this, but merely raised my eyes to the Heavens, while Masou cackled like an old hen.

'And how do we get out of the castle?' asked Ellie, frowning. 'A lady does not leave the castle with the likes of us without the guard stopping her.'

'Then I will be a laundrymaid as well!' I exclaimed, taking her hands. 'I have my old hunting kirtle. It is fit only for walking the dogs since I caught the hem on some brambles. Can you find me an old cloak and hat in the tumblers' clothes chest, Masou?' Masou nodded. 'Now,' I said thoughtfully, 'what business could two laundresses and a tumbler be about in case we are questioned?'

'Well,' began Masou, 'only last month, Mr Somers—'

'We could be gathering nuts!' Ellie butted in.

'Hazelnuts!' I added. 'Picked at dawn to enhance the taste. Well, that is what we shall tell the guard.'

'Maybe so,' said Masou. 'But I was thinking—'

'No, hazelnuts will not do,' I sighed. 'They are not ready for months yet. What else could it be?'

'We could be collecting some early morning dew for washing something,' suggested Ellie.

'The Queen's stockings!' I declared.

'Ladies!' cried Masou loudly. 'I beseech you. Cease your twittering and listen to me. I have a plan and a most simple one.'

'Go on then, Master Knows-all,' said Ellie.

Masou gave us a mocking bow. 'As I was trying to tell you,' he said, 'last month Peter and Paul, the dwarfs, took a horse and cart to Hampton Court Palace. Mr Somers wanted some of those flat, painted trees in the storeroom that were used at the Spring Masque. Hampton Court lies about ten miles south-east from here, so they left early.'

'Thank you, young sir,' I curtsied mockingly. 'I do not know how I would have lived on without knowing about Peter and Paul's most fascinating journey! However, what use it is to us I cannot fathom.'

'By Shaitan's tail!' exclaimed Masou in exasperation. 'Do you not see? We can use the troupe's horse and cart and say we are about the same business.'

'That is brilliant,' I gasped, giving him a hug. 'I should not have been so rude!'

'I think you've both lost your senses,' muttered Ellie. 'We don't want to go to Hampton Court.'

'You misunderstand, sweet Ellie,' said Masou. 'We will only say we are going there. In truth, we shall make for Meadowfold.'

'Oh, I see,' said Ellie slowly. 'Not Hampton Court Palace then?'

'No, Ellie,' smiled Masou. 'Although we can go there afterwards if you wish!'

He darted out of the reach of Ellie as she tried to hit him. I left them chasing round the outside of the Banqueting Hall and went back to join the wedding revels.

Almost immediately, the Queen caught my eye.

'How fare you, my lady?' she asked, as I came to her side. 'Has the pain abated?'

'It has quite abated, My Liege,' I told her. 'I was mistaken in believing it was a matter of any note. Forgive me.'

The Queen dismissed me with a nod. I had no wish to deceive her, but I fear she would have forbidden all my plans if she had known of them.

The feast was magnificent. Much was made of the venison, for it had been killed by Her Majesty some weeks ago. There was also roasted lamb and capons followed by quails and larks. Then we rose and drank to Her Majesty. We lifted our gold cups to her for providing the venison, and then for being the fairest among us and the wisest. The Queen thanked us with a brilliant speech, all in Latin. I understood but little, and when she quizzed me on it later my lack of prowess was evident! Now Penelope and Thomas's health was toasted with white Burgundy wine. Then a toast was called for the repair of Sir John's ankle and another for the coming of May and yet another for St George's Day. We were up and down like jack-in-the-boxes!

Then we progressed to the Banqueting Hall, where the wedding cakes had been prepared. We all watched Penelope and Thomas try to kiss over the mountain of sweet cakes, and it was very funny. Each time they almost touched lips, more cakes would be added to the pile. At one point Penelope complained that she could not see Thomas at all and must needs eat her way to him! (I would not have wanted to eat any of the cakes because those that fell were put upon the heap again and they were battered and covered in rushes.) Thomas ended it all by sweeping the cakes from the table with one arm and grabbing Penelope with the other. The Queen roared with laughter and we all joined in.

Then we returned to St George's Hall, which had been cleared and freshly strewn with rushes for the dancing. I dreaded that Lord Ruxbury would ask me to dance. I was not sure I could keep my countenance, and feared I might find myself gabbling about how clever he had been, and asking where he had hidden the gold, and could he do the pig farmer imitation for me one more time! However, he soon approached me.

'The musicians are beginning a Trenchmore,' he said, with a deep bow. 'Will you partner me, Lady Grace?'

I was struck dumb for an instant. Then I pulled myself together. 'With pleasure, Lord Ruxbury,' I told him. And I danced with him as if I had not a care in the world. I said nothing about the robbery. (See, my noble lord, I can playact almost as well as you!)

'Now that you have seen your friend Thomas married, my lord,' I said as we progressed between the lines of dancers, 'will you remain at Court?'

'I very much hope so,' Lord Ruxbury answered. 'I have found it most rewarding and pray that no business will take me away – at least for a time.'

I was reassured by this. Lord Ruxbury seemed to think he was safe.

'Would you be sorry if I left?' he added mischievously.

'Indeed not,' I smiled. 'For I would still have Mr Naunton to give me riding lessons, dear Lady Knollys to share a jest with and sprightly Sir Pelham Poucher with whom to dance.'

At this point we cast off and followed our separate lines round the outside of the dance. My partner's eyes twinkled as we met again and he took my hand to lead me under the arched arms of the next couple.

'Then I must stay, my lady,' he said, 'and battle to keep my place as your tutor, clown and dance partner.'

The Trenchmore came to an end and Sir Pelham Poucher, of all people, approached.

'One of my rivals is here already!' whispered Lord Ruxbury. 'Do you think I should fight him?'

I had terrible trouble keeping my face straight as Sir Pelham bowed to me.

'Young Lady Grace,' he puffed, red in the face from the effort of walking across the hall. 'I hope you will accompany me in the Pavane.'

Lord Ruxbury handed me over with a comical, woebegone expression that made me want to burst out laughing. Perhaps it was as well that I did not dance with him again.

It was only midnight when the Queen announced that the festivities were over.

'We shall be closeted in our Privy Chamber for the whole of the morning on the morrow,' she announced. 'For it is our duty to deal with matters of State and there has been enough revelry over this wedding to last a month.'

Mrs Champernowne dropped a curtsy. 'The Maids and I will be at your side whenever you wish, My Liege,' she said.

My heart sank. I had not thought about how I would contrive to be from Court in the morning. I could not ask the Queen's permission. She would never let me leave without an escort of guards – and that would not do, for Lord Ruxbury would surely get to hear of it. However, the Queen seemed determined to help me, even if she did not know it!

'We have no wish to be surrounded by giggling Maids who will still have their heads full of these nuptials,' she snapped. 'You must amuse yourselves. Some will wish to take the time to study their Latin.' And she stared hard at me.

This was an excellent notion. The Queen did not want to see me all morning and I could tell Mrs Champernowne that I had to study Latin on Her Majesty's orders, so she would not look for me either!

The whole Court bowed and curtsied as the Queen withdrew, followed by her Ladies-in-Waiting and Maids of Honour. The bride and groom came after us. As we went through the corridors a group of Thomas's friends rushed along and bundled the happy couple away to their bedchamber, as is the custom.

Mrs Champernowne would have none of this and led us away to our own rooms.

Faith! I must get some sleep now, for I have to be up most early for the second day in a row.

The Twenty-fourth Day of April, in the Year of Our Lord 1570

In the Queen's Privy Chamber

This morning has been so exciting. In truth, it has sapped my strength! Now it is early in the afternoon and I am seated by one of the windows of the Queen's Privy Chamber with my feet on a stool – on Her Majesty's express orders. (Orders that were only given after she had exploded like a cask of bad ale when she heard what I had been about!) I was happy to obey, but I did beg my daybooke so that I could make a good report of my morning's work.

The chamber is unusually quiet. There are only two scribes here with me. Her Majesty and the Court are playing bowls in the Tilting Yard and enjoying the spring sunshine. The scribes are both scratching away at some letters of State and are not interested in me in the slightest. They would be agog if they knew of what I was writing. I am very weary and the sun is shining on me, making my eyes want to close, but I must concentrate on my task.

Ellie woke me at sunrise. I almost leaped out of bed with excitement, until I recalled that I must not wake Lady Sarah or Mary Shelton. I quickly dressed in my oldest kirtle. I had worn it last walking the Queen's dogs on a rainy day – so as well as the bramble tears, it was mud-splattered. It was still much finer than anything Ellie wore, but I decided I would pass as a poor serving girl with it hidden under a rough cloak.

We slipped down quietly and met Masou in the Engine Court. He handed us both a cloak and cap. They were rough and smelled of dogs. However, I had my duty to the Queen to think of and I put them on without complaint. Ellie, on the other hand, was delighted to have a cloak and did not seem to mind the animal hairs.

'How do I look?' I demanded.

Masou walked around me with his hand on his chin. 'Hmm,' he said. 'Too tall, too well fed, but fortunately you stink like a dog!'

I tried to slap his arm but he simply darted out of the way. It is true that I am tall for my age and certainly taller than most serving wenches. I crunched up my back as if I had a hump. 'Will this do?' I asked.

Masou, the wretch, was laughing too hard to speak. It fell to Ellie to give me a fair reply.

'That's better, Grace,' she said. 'As long as you remember not to speak to anyone. You know you can only talk like a lady and would be found out in an instant.'

'If you wish to make a habit of disguising yourself,' advised Masou, 'you can do no better than watch a master at work!'

With that he turned away from us. We could not see what he was doing, but when he turned round again he was wearing an old leather hat and a beard! He looked transformed, although I was not going to admit it to him.

''Zounds, Masou!' I said in mock horror, 'You have a rat clinging to your face!'

'Do you not think I look like a proper man?' he asked, sounding annoyed.

'I suppose so,' I had to admit. 'You put me in mind of French Louis. Come, let us go.'

At the Castle Gate I put up my hood and kept my face averted in case the guard should recognize me.

Somehow Masou managed to lower his voice and sound like a man. 'We are on Mr Somers's business,' he said gruffly. 'Some painted artefacts are to be fetched from Hampton Court Palace.'

I held my breath. For an instant I thought the guard was going to challenge us. But it seemed Masou had convinced him, and through we went.

Ellie and I stood a way off from the stables as Masou fetched the horse and cart. I did not want to run the risk of Perkin recognizing me, smelly cloak or no, and Masou would need his help to put Dobbin, the old pony, in the shafts.

Masou led Dobbin down Castle Hill and we followed. Once on the flat, Ellie and I clambered into the back of the cart and waited for Masou to climb up to the driver's seat. But he just stared at it.

'Won't you drive, Grace?' he asked.

'Faith no!' I exclaimed. 'I have no skill at it.'

'Ah,' said Masou, stroking his new beard. 'Then we may have a problem. For I also have never driven a cart, and I cannot risk doing so without gloves. The reins will give me blisters and that will be the end of the best juggler in Mr Somers's troupe.'

'Give me them reins,' declared Ellie stoutly, clambering forwards to sit on the seat at the front. 'We'll be here all day otherwise. After all, how hard can it be?' She flicked the reins. 'Gee up, Dobbin!' she called. Nothing happened. 'How do you make it go?' she muttered.

'I recollect French Louis talking of a slap on the rump with a hat,' said Masou. He took off his hat and flicked the horse with it.

Without warning, Dobbin set off at a fast trot along the south road. I went sprawling in the back of the cart and Masou only just managed to jump in.

'God in Heaven!' wailed Ellie. 'How do you make it stop?'

'Do not even try!' Masou shouted, clinging on for grim death. 'Let us worry about that when we reach Meadowfold.'

I felt as if my teeth were being shaken from my mouth as we jolted along. I will never complain again about riding Doucette. I was just wondering how much I could endure when Dobbin decided to slow to a walk. It seemed that a hit on the rump did not last long in his memory, for Ellie could not entice him to move any faster. She shook the reins but Dobbin just tossed his head in anger so she did not try it again.

Even at that slow pace, the ride was rough. By the time we got near to the crossroads at Meadowfold my bum was so sore I could hardly move.

'The farm's over there,' I called, pointing to the little track that led off to the left.

'That's all very well,' yelped Ellie, 'if that's the way Dobbin chooses.'

She pulled hard on the left rein and for once

Dobbin obliged. The old pony made heavy weather of the rutted track to the tumbledown farm. But then suddenly he livened up and began to trot again.

'Now what's he doing?' wailed Ellie. 'He'll have us in that barn if—'

And at that moment Dobbin stopped! It was so sudden that Masou and I crashed against the driver's bench and poor Ellie tumbled forwards and fell between the shafts. Dobbin had found a clump of tasty cow parsley.

Masou and I clambered down and pulled Ellie to her feet. I think we were all glad to be on safe and steady land.

'I believe Mr Somers has lost his best tumbler,' groaned Masou, 'for I fear henceforth I shall be unable to walk, let alone turn a somersault.'

'I am covered in bruises,' I complained, rubbing my arm. 'And my elbows have no skin left on them.'

'What about me!' demanded Ellie, rubbing her head. 'I fell on me noddle!'

'What luck that it is so hard then, Mistress Ellie!' Masou grinned.

'We must make haste,' I said before Ellie could retaliate. 'First, we must attend to Dobbin. I have learned that much from Perkin. If we do not give him food and water, we will be walking home without him.'

We picked the lushest cow parsley we could find and enticed Dobbin down to a nearby stream so that he would not be seen from the barns. We tethered him there and drank some of the sparkling water ourselves.

'I wish we could eat cow parsley,' sighed Ellie wistfully, 'for I have such a hunger. It must be nigh on nine of the clock by the height of the sun.'

'I too,' I said. 'I did not give any thought to food before we left.'

'You may be a fine Lady Pursuivant, Grace,' said Masou, laughing, 'but you would make a poor general, for the preparation for your campaign has been sorely lacking. 'Tis lucky you have me along.' He reached inside his cloak and produced a small sack. Within it lay three apples and a battered veal pasty. It was the most welcome sight in the world, but we ate hurriedly, for we had to get on with our task and did not want to be discovered.

'Mr Hatton's men made a good search yesterday,' I told my friends, 'but they were after signs of the thief, not the gold. And all they found were the remains of the fire yonder.'

Together we combed the decrepit buildings one after the other. The house was just one room, with a table and bench in the middle and a mouldy palliasse in one corner. There was nowhere to hide a sapphire, let alone a saddlebag. We went on to the barns and poked about among piles of straw and wood, disturbing many a mouse and spider.

'What is this?' cried Masou suddenly. Ellie and I ran to him. The light was very dim in the corner where he crouched, but he seemed to be pulling a heavy leather object out from under some rotten timber.

'Is it a saddlebag?' I gasped. 'Have you found the gold?'

Masou put his hand in. When he drew it out there was a most horrible smell!

'If that be treasure,' said Ellie, holding her

nose, 'I doubt the Queen will want it, for it has curdled!'

'Verily that is so,' agreed Masou, wiping his hand on some straw. 'We have found naught but an old cow bucket. Ladies! Back to the search.'

But we discovered nothing else. At last we stood in the barn where the pig farmer had brought Mr Hatton and his men and looked at each other.

'The gold can't be here at the farm,' said Ellie. She rubbed a grimy hand over her brow. 'We've looked everywhere.'

'It must be here!' I groaned. But I was beginning to doubt it myself. I brought to mind a picture of the pig farmer as he stood in the barn yesterday, his feet in the ashes of the fire. He had not shown a glimmer of fear as Mr Hatton's men searched the place. Indeed, he had not even moved. That must have meant that the gold was in a safe place far away. Or—

'It was under his feet!' I exclaimed suddenly.

'What do you mean?' asked Ellie, puzzled.

'Explain yourself, Grace,' ordered Masou, 'before we believe you have lost your wits!'

'The only place Mr Hatton's men cannot have searched is here!' I told them, pointing to the remains of the fire.

'You are mazed indeed, Grace!' laughed Masou. 'These ashes could not conceal a sausage, let alone a saddlebag!'

'But no one has looked beneath them!' I cried. To my friends' astonishment, I bent down and began to sweep away the ashes with my bare hands. Before long a rusted metal ring appeared.

'A trapdoor!' exclaimed Ellie. 'Looks like a cellar!'

We heaved open the heavy door and looked down into the dark, dank hole.

'We need a light,' I said, 'or we shall see nothing down there.'

'Have no fear' – Masou grinned – 'General Masou has it all in hand! Here are my trusty tinder box and candle.'

Masou lit the candle, and by its flickering light we could see an old wooden ladder with missing rungs leading down beneath the barn. It did not look very safe, but we could not let that stop us.

'I shall go first,' Masou volunteered.

He disappeared into the dark. We could see the flame bobbing as he went. Ellie and I followed. The ladder was not long, but it wobbled horribly and I was glad to get my feet on the hard earth floor below. Masou climbed back up, and scattered some straw and ashes across the trapdoor as he lowered it, sealing us all underground. I wished he did not have to, but we could not risk anyone coming along and realizing we were there.

Ellie had the candle and she held it up so that we could investigate. There was little in the cellar but some broken barrels stacked near a pile of sacks in a corner. There were cobwebs everywhere and a stifling smell of mouldy leaves and wet earth.

''Tis like the grave!' whispered Ellie, shivering. 'I can't stay here.'

'Then we shall be quick,' I told her.

I strode over and pulled the sacks aside.

There was something underneath them! 'Bring the candle,' I squeaked in excitement.

Ellie held the light close. First we came upon a pair of breeches and a jerkin that stank of brandy. Then we uncovered a battered hat and a smelly smock. I realized that these were the clothes of the drunkard and the pig farmer! We had found Lord Ruxbury's disguises!

Wrinkling her nose, Ellie lifted them up to reveal something else. In the flickering candlelight we could just make out the ornate stitching and delicate workmanship of two fine leather saddlebags!

With trembling hands I struggled to undo the stiff buckle on one of the bags. At last it came free; the bag opened and its contents spilled out onto the floor. We all gasped, for pearls and diamonds, rubies and gold littered the ground and sparkled in the candlelight.

'God's truth!' breathed Ellie. 'There's a queen's ransom here!'

'We must make haste and get this to Her Majesty,' I said.

We hurriedly scooped the jewels and coins

back into their leather bag and fastened it shut. Then we heaved both bags to the bottom of the ladder. It was going to be very hard to get our heavy load up and out of the cellar.

At that moment I heard a sound. Someone was walking across the floor above!

'Hide!' I hissed. Without delay we dragged the saddlebags behind the barrels and crouched down with them. Masou pinched out the candle and we huddled together nervously.

The trapdoor creaked open and a lantern appeared at the opening. My thoughts were in a fever. Surely this could not be Lord Ruxbury! He was back at Court and had no idea that he was even suspected. Mayhap it was someone from Meadowfold who had heard about the pig farmer and knew there was no such fellow. They could have come to look for the gold themselves. Then I had a terrible thought. Did Lord Ruxbury have an accomplice after all? Someone who might not hesitate to fire a gun! I tried not to breathe and I think Masou and Ellie were doing the same.

I could see nothing from my hiding place,

but I heard someone climb quickly down the ladder and make straight for the pile of sacks. Then there was a deep, muffled curse; the stranger must have discovered that the saddle-bags were missing.

Then the light seemed to swing round and a huge shadow moved across the wall above our heads. I could hear the blood pounding in my ears. Were we going to be discovered? Ellie's hand crept into mine. The next few minutes felt like long hours. I waited for the lantern to shine in my face. It drew closer for a moment, and then, to my huge relief, I heard footsteps going up the ladder. The trapdoor was slammed shut and we were left in darkness.

Masou let out a deep breath. 'I thought we would be found for sure,' he gasped. 'Allah be praised! Whoever it was must have believed that the gold was long gone.'

'What do we do now?' whispered Ellie.

'We must bide our time in case he is still about,' I told them. 'But I think it would be safe to light the candle again.'

I felt better with the feeble light from the

candle stub, yet we did not dare move from behind the barrels for several minutes.

At last Masou crept out. 'We cannot stay here all day,' he whispered. 'I will make certain that our visitor has departed.' He slowly climbed the ladder and listened intently.

'Be careful, Masou,' I warned.

He cautiously opened the trapdoor a crack and peered through. 'I cannot see a soul,' he muttered. ''Tis time to be bold.' He pushed the trapdoor up and put his head through the hole. I was terrified that someone would suddenly grab him, but the seconds passed and nothing happened. Finally he climbed out into the barn and a few moments later he threw the trapdoor completely open.

His grinning face appeared at the opening. 'There is no one about,' he announced.

'Then we have no time to lose,' I said. 'I am heartily sick of this place. Let us make haste for Windsor.'

'How are we going to get the gold out?' asked Ellie, trying to lift one of the bags. 'It's mighty heavy.'

'Mayhap we should have asked our visitor to help us before he left!' laughed Masou. 'But as he has gone, Dobbin will have to lend us his leading rope. We can use that as a hoist, for 'twill be easier to pull the saddlebags up than carry them. I saw many heavy water buckets raised from the river that way when I was a boy in Africa.'

Masou's trick with the rope worked well, although we still had to use all our strength to pull the bags out of the cellar. We lugged them onto the cart and covered them with broken pieces of timber.

'What will the guard at the castle gate say to all these woodwormy planks?' I wondered aloud.

'Fear not, dear Grace,' responded Masou. 'My nimble brain will think of something.'

We set off for the Windsor road. We had to hurry but Dobbin did not seem to feel the need to rush. Hitting him on the rump with a hat no longer seemed to get him started. Masou managed to get him moving at last by going ahead with some cow parsley, but all the pony would do was a slow walk.

''Twill be midnight by the time we reach the castle!' I exclaimed. 'And we will have run out of dandelions by then. Is there nothing else we can try?'

Masou frowned in thought. 'There is some silly song or other that French Louis sings to Dobbin,' he said at last. '*Le Canard Fait Coincoin* – I think that is the one. I wonder if it would work.'

And it did work. We sang all the way back to Windsor Castle, and Dobbin picked up the pace and even broke into a trot occasionally. By the time we arrived I was heartily sick of the duck that said 'quack-quack'!

'Cart for Mr Somers!' growled Masou in his deep voice when we reached the castle gate. The guard looked doubtfully at our load of wormy wood, and I hoped that Masou had got his excuse ready, for I had none.

'My master has need of this for a dramatic tableau of a terrible shipwreck,' Masou said quickly.

'Methinks your master has sent you on a

fool's errand!' sneered the guard as he waved us through. 'There's wood aplenty in the Great Park.'

Masou jumped down and led Dobbin across the Tilting Yard and through to the Kitchen Court. Ellie and I climbed down from the cart, groaning from the stiffness of our limbs.

'What shall we do with the gold?' asked Ellie in a whisper.

'We will leave it here under the wood,' I replied, looking round to make sure we were not overheard. 'Masou will hide and watch it, but he must not be found with it for he will be thought the thief. You get back to your work. As soon as I have transformed myself into a Maid of Honour again, I shall alert the Queen.'

Masou took up his post of keeping secret watch on the cart, while I made haste to my bedchamber. There I wiped the grime from my hands as best I could, quickly changed into my simplest chemise and kirtle (for I had no one to help me tie on sleeves) and then made for the Presence Chamber.

As always, the Queen was surrounded by courtiers. They were listening to a group of Venetian musicians playing sackbuts and crumhorns. I could see no sign of Lord Ruxbury. Her Majesty looked up as I approached.

'Freed from the Latin primer at last, Grace?' she said as I made a curtsy before her. 'I was most surprised to hear from Mrs Champernowne that you spent your whole morning thus.'

'I would beg a moment of your time, Your Majesty,' I said, looking steadily at her. 'For my morning has been most *profitably* spent and I will *treasure* the hours that have passed. They are worth their weight in gold!'

Without a word, Her Majesty rose and took me firmly by the arm. She swept me through the crowds, who bowed as we passed, and I caught a glimpse of Carmina's startled face. Behind me I could hear the musicians falter. 'Play on!' roared the Queen over her shoulder. 'I shall return directly.' She pushed me into her Privy Chamber, waving away her servants and the guards who had followed us. She slammed the doors shut.

'Now what is this all about, my stubborn lady?' demanded the Queen. 'I imagine you allude to the matter of my missing gold. But I am tired of hearing of it and had thought your investigation finished!'

'Your Gracious Majesty is right,' I said, trying not to smile. 'All is at an end. If you will come with me to the window, I shall show you where your gold is to be found.' We walked over and looked down into the Kitchen Court. I pointed to the cart. 'Underneath the wood lie two saddlebags,' I said.

'You speak in riddles, Grace!' retorted the Queen. 'What have saddlebags to do with my gold?'

I found myself hesitating. I almost wished I could hand Her Majesty's gold back to her without giving away the name of the thief. If only he had not stolen the Queen's money, she would have loved to hear about the exploits of this daring robber. When I thought of him I wanted to smile, but I did not think Her Majesty would be very pleased with me if I did!

'They belong to Lord Ruxbury,' I explained. 'And they are crammed full of your stolen jewels and coins. Lord Ruxbury was the thief.'

'I can hardly believe this is so, Grace,' the Queen said, looking at me with puzzlement and concern in her eyes.

'Your Majesty, I beg you to trust your Lady Pursuivant,' I urged her. 'Ask your guard but to fetch the saddlebags and you will know that my words are true.'

Her Majesty stared hard at me. Then she nodded and took my hands. 'You have never failed me yet, Grace,' she said. She strode to the doors and flung them open. 'Get you to the cart in the Tilting Yard, search under the wood, and bring back what you find!' she shouted at the guards. 'And we would have Lord Ruxbury fetched immediately.'

Of course, Lord Ruxbury must be brought to justice, but he had only taken a little of the Queen's gold and he had not hurt anyone – apart from giving two guards a bit of a headache. I did not want to think of what his punishment might be.

We returned to the Presence Chamber, where the Queen waved the musicians to silence and summoned Mr Hatton to her side. They had a murmured conversation and Mr Hatton turned pale, while the rest of the Court stood and shuffled their feet. I could tell everyone was agog with curiosity but no one dared speak. Before long the guards returned, carrying the saddlebags. They bowed to the Queen.

'Show us what is within them,' ordered Her Majesty. 'And make haste!'

The saddlebags were quickly opened and their contents tipped onto the floor. A gasp of wonder went round the Court at the sight of the treasure, and the Queen's face broke into a huge smile.

'That which was lost has been found,' she announced. 'And the thief is being brought to us even now.'

All around me I could hear excited whispers and murmured conversations about who the thief could be. And then two more guards came in and bowed deeply.

'There is no sign of Lord Ruxbury, My Liege,' said one. 'His room is empty and his mare is not in the stables.' At the mention of the thief's name, another gasp of wonder went round the Court.

I had to keep myself from grinning at the guard's news. I should never have doubted Lord Ruxbury would keep one step ahead of us all. He must have known he was discovered once he found his gold missing, for now I was in no doubt that it had been he who came to the cellar beneath the barn this morning, as Ellie, Masou and I hid behind the barrels.

'Damn him to Hell!' shouted the Queen. 'He must not get away!'

'The Gentlemen of the Guard will seek him out,' Mr Hatton assured her.

'See that they do so and right swiftly!' demanded Her Majesty, as Mr Hatton left with his men. Then the Queen turned to the musicians. 'Play on,' she said, 'and I shall attend to my errant Maid. Come, Grace, I would hear your . . . Latin.'

Back in her Privy Chamber, I told the

Queen the whole story. She swung between immense anger at my folly and sheer delight at the outcome of the matter. When I had finished my tale, she directed me to the chair where I am sitting now, and ordered some mead and manchet bread to be brought directly.

But before I could allow myself to eat, I had to find out if Ellie had been able to make a good account of her absence. 'Your Majesty,' I said, kneeling down before her, 'I was helped in my endeavour by Ellie the laundrymaid and Masou the tumbler and would not have succeeded without them. While Mr Somers is a kind master, Ellie will not receive the same kindness from Mrs Fadget. I fear she will be unable to explain her absence, for she is loyal to Your Majesty and will keep my secret.'

'What would you have me say to Mrs Fadget, Grace?' asked the Queen solemnly. 'Shall I tell her that Ellie has been immured with her Latin tutor all the while?' Then she smiled and patted my hand. 'Have no fear, my dear god-daughter. I will speak to this unkind starching woman.'

Ellie and Mrs Fadget were summoned. Mrs Fadget soon appeared, dragging poor Ellie along with her. The Deputy Laundress wore a nasty smirk on her face and I believe she thought the Queen had called her to witness some punishment for Ellie.

'Mrs Fadget,' said Her Majesty, as they knelt before her, 'we must congratulate you on having such worthy staff. Young Ellie Bunting here has been busy on our business all the day without a meal or a rest and yet we warrant not a word of complaint has passed her lips.' I wanted to giggle as I saw the smirk disappear from Mrs Fadget's face. 'You are to take her straight to the kitchen and see she is fed and fed well. Then she is to rest. We would not have her about her duties again until tomorrow.' Mrs Fadget's lips moved as if to protest. 'And remember, mistress, we have eyes everywhere and will know how you deal with her.'

Mrs Fadget looked fearfully around the

chamber as if she expected to see eyes peering at her from the walls. I believe that Ellie will be safe from her temper – for the time being at least. She ushered out the stunned Ellie as if she were her own daughter!

When they had gone the Queen looked at me. 'I must thank you, my dear Lady Pursuivant, for the return of my gold. I can always trust to your loyalty even if I cannot trust to the loyalty of some of my subjects. Now, you are pale after all your exertions on my behalf. Eat and drink your fill and then I insist you rest here. You will be quiet.'

I fell upon the food and the Queen chuckled at the sight. Then I asked for my daybooke and—

Hell's teeth! I nearly nodded off just then in the warm sunshine from the window. I only just caught my inkpot! I will seek Her Majesty's permission to return to my bedchamber and sleep.

In Her Majesty's Presence Chamber

It is almost sundown and I am sitting quietly with the other Maids of Honour and the Ladies-in-Waiting in the Queen's Presence Chamber. Her Majesty told the assembled Court at supper that we were the only companions she desired this evening. She has declared that she wants no more to do with men, 'for they are naught but villains who make off with either our Maids or our gold!' she announced. This will only last until tomorrow, when she has the first sniff of flattery from some silly courtier!

I am glad there is no revelry tonight. I can sit here and write while everyone else reads quietly and Her Majesty stares gloomily straight ahead, a hand to her cheek. Her pleasure over her recovered gold has gone for the moment. Nobody dares move except to turn a page. I am straining every nerve not to let my quill scratch loudly on the page of my daybooke, for I am sure to be in trouble if I do!

We are supposed to believe the Queen's ill temper is due to Penelope's absence, for she left for Staffordshire while I was at Meadowfold. In truth Her Majesty whispered to me that she has a toothache, but she will not admit it to the others.

After my last entry I went straight back to my bedchamber to sleep and found it full of Maids! No sooner had I opened the door than Lady Jane, Mary Shelton and Carmina fell upon me.

'Where have you been, Grace?' demanded Carmina. 'You were not at breakfast, and no one could find you for hours!'

'We were told you were studying Latin,' added Lady Jane, 'which we found most hard to believe!'

'You missed Penelope's departure,' put in Mary Shelton.

'Then you appeared in the Presence Chamber,' Carmina gabbled, her eyes dancing with excitement, 'and were whisked away by the Queen, and then you returned and then you were taken off again! And we find that dashing Lord Ruxbury is also an audacious thief!'

'So the robber was not a sturdy beggar, as Mr Hatton thought,' added Mary.

'No, indeed!' gasped Carmina, gazing into the distance. 'For Lord Ruxbury is handsome and courteous and he outwitted the guards with his cleverness. It is hard to think ill of him.'

'He was a fine figure on that beautiful mare of his,' agreed Mary.

'All the ladies have said so!' sighed Carmina. 'How could he have done such a thing?'

'Perchance you are privy to what happened, Grace?' Mary enquired.

I knew I could not get away without telling the tale. 'Indeed, I do have some knowledge of the trouble,' I said. 'The Queen has explained to me the gist of the matter – and it is astonishing indeed!'

Mary Shelton and Carmina listened wide-eyed as I told them the story of Lord Ruxbury's daring theft of the Queen's gold. Of course, I had to leave out my own involvement and give all the credit to Mr Hatton and his men! It was most galling! However, I did enjoy describing the discovery of the haul at Meadowfold – though I made it sound as if it were the Gentlemen of the Guard who had been there and not me.

'Yet I bid you tell no one,' I finished, 'for Her Majesty wants an end to the matter.' This was not a tale that could be spread around.

'You have the gift of the storyteller, Grace!' breathed Carmina. 'You make it sound as if you were actually there!'

'What an idea!' I exclaimed, blushing as I realized that my enthusiasm had carried me a little too far. 'A mere Maid of Honour on such an adventure! But it is Her Majesty you should be complimenting if my story pleases. She painted so vivid a picture that I saw it all in my mind's eye as she spoke.'

It was lucky that Lady Jane broke in at that point. 'I see no great delights in the tale,' she said stiffly. 'The gold has been recovered and that's an end to it! Would that I had a fraction of the Queen's wealth – then I should not have troubled myself with a worthless courtier who cannot keep from making foolish wagers at the card table.'

'So Mr Naunton failed in his promise to desist from his betting?' I asked, hoping she would spare me the details.

'I am done with Mr Naunton for ever!' exclaimed Lady Jane, as if she would take herself off to pine away and die like a swan that has lost its mate. I could hardly keep my face straight at her pained expression. I knew that she had at least three other courtiers lining up for her and had been keeping them on strings just in case.

'Try to forget him and think of pleasant things,' urged Mary kindly. 'Your sadness will pass.'

'Indeed,' agreed Carmina, who seemingly could not wait to return to the tale of the vanished Lord Ruxbury. 'What more has the Queen told you of the theft, Grace?'

'And where does Mr Hatton think the villain has gone?' asked Mary eagerly.

I noticed that even Lady Jane looked interested at that.

'I know only this,' I told them. 'Lord Ruxbury was most clever and may now be in the guise of a prince or a pauper. I think we shall never find him. He could be anywhere!'

At that moment the door to the bed-chamber opened with a bang. We all jumped but it was only Lady Sarah. She swept in, holding a piece of linen to her forehead.

'I cannot rid myself of this wretched spot!' she complained as she dabbed a tincture of something smelly onto the place. 'It is most vexing!' Suddenly she caught sight of me. 'Grace! You are here! Fie upon you for vanishing from your bed so early. Upon my life I have been worrying all morning!' Clearly this was not true – unless she meant that she had been worrying about her appearance. I was about to apologize for alarming her, but she continued, 'And I was not alone. Lord Ruxbury asked where you were at breakfast and I could not give him a fair answer.'

'I was with my Latin tutor,' I told her.

'Well, no one thought to inform me!' said Lady Sarah. 'So I told Lord Ruxbury that you were likely off on one of your madcap schemes.'

I opened my mouth to protest – madcap schemes indeed! But Lady Sarah had now unravelled the last thread of the mystery. I had not completely covered my tracks, and that is why Lord Ruxbury had gone to check on his gold.

And I couldn't help being glad that he had realized I was on to him, for it had given him a chance to escape punishment.

'What ails you, Grace?' asked Mary. 'You are lost in thought.'

'I am just tired after my morning of . . . Latin,' I told her hurriedly. And while the other Maids twittered on about Lord Ruxbury – how handsome he was and what a marvellous horseman and, of course, how wicked to steal the Queen's gold (though I could tell they would have forgiven him in return for one smile!) – I curled up on my bed and shut my eyes. And the next thing I knew we were being called to supper.

At supper everyone was gossiping about Lord Ruxbury – who has not been found. All except Her Majesty, of course, who just shouted curses on his head whenever his name was mentioned. So it was not – in her hearing.

Carmina has heard, from a cousin of Thomas Penn, that Lord Ruxbury has huge estates in France that his father left in terrible debt, and this is probably why he stole the gold. The other stories of Lord Ruxbury are more wondrous and likely untrue. He has been accused of every crime that has taken place in the last year, from apple stealing to murder. Sir Pelham Poucher declared that he himself saw the villain making for the road to Scotland, and was loudly contradicted by Henry Westerland, who believed Lord Ruxbury had boarded a ship for Spain and was going to relieve King Philip of his jewels! Mrs Champernowne is sure that he is just a common thief who only pretended to be noble, while Ellie had it from Mrs Fadget that Lord Ruxbury is, in truth, the King of the Fairies, who came among us mortals on his black steed only intent on making mischief.

I think he was human enough. The tale I like most came from Perkin, by way of Mary Shelton. He believes that Lord Ruxbury has gone to Europe, where he will earn his living by displays of horsemanship. In truth I have heard there is talk of a riding school being founded in Vienna, and Lord Ruxbury is a fine teacher, so perchance could make a good life there. I can imagine he and Minstrel would live quite happily in this manner. And I hope they do. Lord Ruxbury was wrong to steal the Queen's gold, but I cannot believe he is a thoroughly wicked man, nor can I be sorry that he escaped and will not be punished for his crime; shame on the Queen's own Lady Pursuivant!

Now my daybooke is nearly full. Tonight I will hide it away until Penelope is next at Court, for there are a few passages I can read to her. Strange to think that just a few days ago the wedding was the only thing I imagined I would be writing about! Little did I dream that—

Hell's teeth! The Queen is glaring at my scratchy quill. I must stop.

In my bedchamber

Something very strange has just happened and I have had to dig this daybooke out again, for I must record what took place not five minutes ago as it pertains to the same mystery.

Mary Shelton and I had left the noontide meal and come to our chamber, for my skirts were badly stained with wine and I needed to change. (It was not my fault. My sleeve caught my goblet as I reached for some bread.) I was standing there in my partlet and petticoat when there was a knocking at the door.

'Perchance that is Fran come to help,' said Mary. She went to the door and had a few muttered words with someone while I started to climb into my fresh gown.

Soon Mary closed the door and turned to me. 'That was odd,' she said, holding out a parcel wrapped in lilac linen and tied with a ribbon. 'It was an old serving woman with this for you, Grace. She claimed she had been told to leave it in your chamber.'

I took it from her. 'What can it be?' I mused. 'Which servant was it?'

'I do not know,' said Mary, puzzled, 'though in truth I did not see much of her face, for she had her shawl pulled up around her head. Her voice was throaty and gruff and I did not recognize it. Come, open your parcel and show me what it is.'

I sat on my bed and undid the ribbon. Inside was a beautiful daybooke with a soft vellum cover. I opened it to find an inscription on the first page:

To a clever young lady,
I thought my hand unbeatable, but you held
all the trumps.
I dare to hope that one day our paths may
cross again.
R

I threw the book down and pulled my gown up to cover me as I ran to the door and flung it open. I looked frantically up and down the passage but there was no one there. I felt a huge pang of disappointment, for I had guessed that the figure at the door had not been a serving woman, but Lord Ruxbury himself in another disguise!

'What is the matter?' Mary Shelton asked in surprise.

'I simply wished to thank the messenger,' I told her in a fluster.

'But who sent the gift?' Mary wanted to know.

'Er . . . Her Majesty,' I faltered. 'She saw that I had almost finished my last daybooke and had this one delivered to me.'

'That was kind,' smiled Mary. 'Now stand still while I lace your sleeve.'

She helped me finish dressing and made to go back to the dinner table. I said I would follow shortly. I told her I was going to compose a thank you in Latin for the Queen. But in truth I needed to record the last twist in the tale. As soon as Mary had gone I pulled out this old daybooke to make my final entry.

My thoughts are whirling like snowflakes in a storm. Lord Ruxbury came back to Windsor Castle! He put himself in terrible danger, and all to give me a gift! He must hold me in high regard, and that thought gives me a warm feeling in my heart so that I cannot stop smiling.

Even now he could be within the walls of Windsor Castle. I suppose I ought to alert the guards, yet I do not think I shall. All I would achieve is the further upset of Her Majesty as her palace is turned upside down while the guards search for Lord Ruxbury again. And anyway, by the time I find someone to tell, Lord Ruxbury and Minstrel will be galloping away, too fast to be caught.

I doubt I will ever see them again. But I know this: I will never forget Lord Ruxbury and his beautiful black mare.

And now I must return to St George's Hall and the dining table. Faith! I am glad I do not really have to compose a note to the Queen in Latin. I would not get further than 'O Supremus Majestatem' – and I am not even certain that is right!

GLOSSARY

aiglet – the metal tip of a lace, which you thread through the hole

Almain – a stately sixteenth century dance

arras – a tapestry hung on the wall

beshrew – express disapproval of

bodice – the top part of a woman's dress

bum – bottom

bumroll – a sausage-shaped piece of padding worn round the hips to make them look bigger

casket – a small decorative box

chemise – a loose shirt-like undergarment

clothes press – a large storage cupboard

copper – usually a copper saucepan or cauldron used for cooking

crumhorn – a wind instrument shaped like an umbrella's handle

Cuckoo-pint roots – the roots of the alum plant, which resembles the potato but is highly poisonous

daybooke – a book in which you would record your sins each day so that you could pray about them. The idea of keeping a diary or journal grew out of this. Grace is using hers as a journal

farthingale – a bell- or barrel-shaped petticoat held out with hoops of whalebone

forepart – the part of the garment that covers the chest

harbinger – somebody who went ahead to announce the monarch

honour – a bow, curtsy or series of bows or curtsies at the end of a dance to acknowledge your partner

Janus – the Roman god of beginnings and endings, depicted with two faces or heads because he was able to see in both directions. He gave his name to the month January, which looks forward to the new year and back to the old

jerkin – a close-fitting, hip-length, usually sleeveless jacket

kirtle – the skirt section of an Elizabethan dress

Knights of the Garter – the oldest British Order of Chivalry, reserved as the highest reward for loyalty or military merit. It is said to have got its name from when a countess dropped her garter while dancing with King Edward III

Lady-in-Waiting – one of the ladies who helped to look after the Queen and who kept her company

lead – lead carbonate, used for make-up

Maid of Honour – a younger girl who helped to look after the Queen like a Lady-in-Waiting

manchet bread – white bread

marchpane – marzipan

Mary Shelton – one of Queen Elizabeth's Maids of Honour (a Maid of Honour of this name really did exist, see below). Most Maids of Honour were not officially 'ladies' (like Lady Grace) but they had to be of born of gentry

masque – a masquerade, a masked ball

mead – an alcoholic drink made with honey

medlar – a fruit with a taste similar to a pear

palliasse – a thin mattress

partlet – a very fine embroidered false top, which covered just the shoulders and the upper chest

Pavane – slow and stately dance

poppy syrup – a medicine for inducing sleep

Presence Chamber – the room where Queen Elizabeth would receive people

Privy Chamber – the room where the Queen would receive people in private

pursuivant – one who pursues someone else

Queen's Guard – these were more commonly known as the Gentlemen Pensioners – young noblemen who guarded the Queen from physical attacks

sackbut – an early form of the trombone

Secretary Cecil – William Cecil, an administrator for the Queen (was later made Lord Burghley)

Shaitan – the Islamic word for Satan, though it means a trickster and a liar rather than the ultimate evil

stomacher – a heavily embroidered or jewelled piece for the centre front of a bodice

sweetmeats – sweets

tabard – a sleeveless garment emblazoned with the Queen's coat of arms

tabor – a small drum

ten-day-old urine – ten-day-old urine was used in the laundry for removing stubborn stains!

Tilting Yard – area where knights in armour would joust or 'tilt' (i.e. ride at each other on horseback with lances)

tinder box – small box containing some quick-burning tinder, a piece of flint, a piece of steel and a candle for making fire and thus light

tiring woman – a woman who helped a lady to dress

Trenchmore – a boisterous Irish dance

tumbler – acrobat

tussie-mussie – a little tied posy of sweet-smelling herbs carried by a bridesmaid

Volta – a sixteenth-century dance very popular with Queen Elizabeth I

want-wit – fool

'Zounds – an expression of surprise or annoyance originating from the shortening of 'God's wounds'

In 1485 Queen Elizabeth I's grandfather, Henry Tudor, won the battle of Bosworth Field against Richard III and took the throne of England. He was known as Henry VII. He had two sons, Arthur and Henry. Arthur died while still a boy, so when Henry VII died in 1509, Elizabeth's father came to the throne and England got an eighth king called Henry – the notorious one who had six wives.

Wife number one – Catherine of Aragon – gave Henry one daughter called Mary (who was brought up as a Catholic), but no living sons. To Henry VIII this was a disaster, because nobody believed a queen could ever govern England. He needed a male heir.

Henry wanted to divorce Catherine so he could marry his pregnant mistress, Anne Boleyn. The Pope, the head of the Catholic Church, wouldn't allow him to annul his marriage, so Henry broke with the Catholic Church and set up the Protestant Church of England – or the Episcopal Church, as it's known in the USA.

Wife number two – Anne Boleyn – gave Henry another daughter, Elizabeth (who was brought up as a Protestant). When Anne then miscarried a baby boy, Henry decided he'd better get somebody new, so he accused Anne of infidelity and had her executed.

Wife number three – Jane Seymour – gave Henry a son called Edward, and died of childbed fever a couple of weeks later.

Wife number four – Anne of Cleves – had no children. It was a diplomatic marriage and Henry didn't fancy her, so she agreed to a divorce (wouldn't you?).

Wife number five – Catherine Howard – had no children either. Like Anne Boleyn, she was accused of infidelity and executed.

Wife number six – Catherine Parr – also had no children. She did manage to outlive Henry, though, but only by the skin of her teeth. Nice guy, eh?

Henry VIII died in 1547, and in accordance with the rules of primogeniture (whereby the first-born son inherits from his father), the person who succeeded him was the boy Edward. He became Edward VI. He was strongly Protestant, but died young in 1553.

Next came Catherine of Aragon's daughter, Mary, who became Mary I, known as Bloody Mary. She was strongly Catholic, married Philip II of Spain in a diplomatic match, but died childless five years later. She also burned a lot of Protestants for the good of their souls.

Finally, in 1558, Elizabeth came to the throne. She reigned until her death in 1603. She played the marriage game – that is, she kept a lot of important and influential men hanging on in hopes of marrying her – for a long time. At one time it looked as if she would marry her favourite, Robert Dudley, Earl of Leicester. She didn't though, and I think she probably never intended to get married – would you, if you'd had a dad like hers? So she never had any children.

She was an extraordinary and brilliant woman, and during her reign, England first started to become important as a world power. Sir Francis Drake sailed round the world –

raiding the Spanish colonies of South America for loot as he went. And one of Elizabeth's favourite courtiers, Sir Walter Raleigh, tried to plant the first English colony in North America – at the site of Roanoke in 1585. It failed, but the idea stuck.

The Spanish King Philip II tried to conquer England in 1588. He sent a huge fleet of 150 ships, known as the Invincible Armada, to do it. It failed miserably – defeated by Drake at the head of the English fleet – and most of the ships were wrecked trying to sail home. There were many other great Elizabethans, too – including William Shakespeare and Christopher Marlowe.

After her death, Elizabeth was succeeded by James VI of Scotland, who became James I of England and Scotland. He was almost the last eligible person available! He was the son of Mary Queen of Scots, who was Elizabeth's cousin, via Henry VIII's sister.

His son was Charles I – the King who was beheaded after losing the English Civil War.

★

The stories about Lady Grace Cavendish are set in the years 1569 and 1570, when Elizabeth was thirty-six and still playing the marriage game for all she was worth. The Ladies-in-Waiting and Maids of Honour at her Court weren't servants – they were companions and friends, supplied from upper-class families. Not all of them were officially 'ladies' – only those with titled husbands or fathers; in fact, many of them were unmarried younger daughters sent to Court to find themselves a nice rich lord to marry.

All the Lady Grace Mysteries are invented, but some of the characters in the stories are real people – Queen Elizabeth herself, of course, and Mrs Champernowne and Mary Shelton as well. There never was a Lady Grace Cavendish (as far as we know!) – but there were plenty of girls like her at Elizabeth's Court. The real Mary Shelton foolishly made fun of the Queen herself on one occasion – and got slapped in the face by Elizabeth for her trouble! But most of the time, the Queen seems to have been protective and kind to her Maids of Honour. She was very strict about boyfriends, though. There was one simple rule for boyfriends in those days: you couldn't have one. No boyfriends at all. You would get married to a person your parents chose for you and that was that. Of course, the girls often had other ideas!

Later on in her reign, the Queen had a full-scale secret service run by her great spymaster, Sir Francis Walsingham. His men, who hunted down priests and assassins, were called 'pursuivants'. There are also tantalizing hints that Elizabeth may have had her own personal sources of information – she certainly was very well informed, even when her counsellors tried to keep her in the dark. And who knows whom she might have recruited to find things out for her? There may even have been a Lady Grace Cavendish, after all!

A note on weddings

It might surprise you to know that in Elizabeth I's reign the legal age for marriage was fourteen for boys and just twelve for girls! But in fact many people waited until their twenties. Like nowadays, a Tudor wedding was a time for celebration.

First there was the engagement, or hand fasting. This was a ceremony in which the couple promised to marry each other soon. It was usually conducted by a priest, and the couple would exchange presents. The future bridegroom might give his love a ring, but it could also be a bracelet, or gloves! And afterwards there was a feast, just like an engagement party of today.

A few weeks later the couple got married. There was no choice about where you got married. You couldn't pop in to a handy registry office or fly off to a tropical island. For ordinary people it was the local church or nothing. Guests generally wore their best clothes. The bride did not wear white and only had a new dress if she could afford it. Her bridesmaids would be dressed as finely as they could. Just as now, they often wore gowns in the same colour and style. The bridesmaids were usually in charge of making all the tussie-mussies and the bride's garland of herbs and flowers.

On the day of the wedding everyone walked the bride and groom to the church. This was a noisy business! According to Thomas Becon, who was writing at the time, the party sometimes began before the ceremony had started, so some guests turned up late and very drunk! Can you imagine going to a wedding where a whole crowd of people suddenly burst in playing harps, lutes and drums?

Just like today, the groom's family and friends stood on the right and the bride's on the left. This is an old custom from long before Tudor times. If two families didn't get on, a wedding was a way of bringing peace to the two sides – but they wouldn't go as far as to stand next to each other!

If there were no interruptions from drunken friends, the service was quite solemn and the words used were not so different from those used today. Usually the bride was given a ring to wear on her left hand. But some poorer couples could not afford a ring at all. It didn't matter in a small village where everyone knew you were married.

Mrs Champernowne was not unusual in believing the superstitions of the day. Some were very strange. For instance it was considered good luck to find a spider in your wedding dress! On the other hand it was bad luck to see an open grave on the way to the wedding. (It would certainly have been bad luck if you fell in!)

After the wedding there would be a great party. In richer families this could go on for days with masques and entertainments. The wedding cake was a pile of small cakes for the bride and groom to kiss over, just like Penelope and Thomas's. Sometimes the cakes were thrown at the happy couple for good luck! This tradition carried on until 1660 when a French chef, visiting the court of King Charles II, was so disgusted by the waste of cakes that he went home and designed the iced, tiered cake that we know today.

If you enjoyed this
Lady Grace Mystery,
there are many other
books featuring the
intrepid Lady Grace
for you to explore!

THE LADY GRACE MYSTERIES
ASSASSIN

By Grace Cavendish

MURDER AT COURT!

One suitor dead and another under suspicion – and Lady Grace didn't even *want* to get married! Can Grace, Queen Elizabeth's favourite Maid of Honour, solve the mystery and bring peace back to the Queen's Court?

Open up the daybooke of Lady Grace for a tale of daggers, death and a very daring girl . . .

DOUBLEDAY
0 385 60644 3

THE LADY GRACE MYSTERIES
BETRAYAL

By Grace Cavendish

MYSTERY AT SEA!

Life as a stowaway on board an Elizabethan galleon – it's no place for a lady! But when her fellow Maid of Honour disappears with a dashing sea captain, Lady Grace knows she just has to investigate.

Hide away with the daybooke of Lady Grace, Queen Elizabeth's favourite Maid of Honour, for a tale of high waves and high adventure.

DOUBLEDAY
0 385 60645 1

THE LADY GRACE MYSTERIES
CONSPIRACY

By Grace Cavendish

SUSPICION AND BLOODSHED!

The Royal Court is on its summer travels
and Lady Grace is sure something strange is
going on. As Queen Elizabeth narrowly
escapes a series of mysterious accidents,
Grace must investigate just who might be
behind the conspiracy. Could it really be
one of the Queen's faithful friends – or
even her latest suitor?

Delve into the daybooke of Lady
Grace, Queen Elizabeth's favourite
Maid of Honour, to discover a deadly
dangerous plot . . .

DOUBLEDAY
0 385 60646 X

THE LADY GRACE MYSTERIES
DECEPTION

By Grace Cavendish

DEATH ON THE ICE!

The river Thames has frozen over, and
Lady Grace can't wait to skate down to the
Frost Fair. But a gruesome discovery on
the ice interrupts the winter revelry. Could
the dead body with the coins on its eyes be
connected to problems with the Queen's
new currency? Lady Grace must unravel the
mystery and track down the master forgers
before it's too late . . .

Discover a world of counterfeiting
and corruption inside the daybooke
of Lady Grace.

DOUBLEDAY
0 385 60849 7

THE LADY GRACE MYSTERIES
FEUD

By Grace Cavendish

POISONOUS PLOTS!

The Queen's portrait painters are at court,
bearing exotic colours with deadly
ingredients. Lady Grace is fascinated by the
work of the artists, especially when she
begins to suspect there is a poisoner at
work. Could the paints – or one of the
painters – be to blame?

Piece together the courtly clues within
the daybooke of Lady Grace.

DOUBLEDAY
0 385 60851 9

THE LADY GRACE MYSTERIES
EXILE

By Grace Cavendish

MAGIC AND MAYHEM!

There's a new arrival at Court. Banoo
Yasmine has a pet panther and is rumoured
to have magical powers. Yasmine also owns
the renowned Heart of Kings ruby. When
the famed jewel goes missing, the finger is
pointed at one of Grace's friends.
Can Grace find the true thief?

Lose yourself in the fascinating life of Court
in the daybooke of Lady Grace.

DOUBLEDAY
0 385 60850 0

COMING SOON!

THE LADY GRACE MYSTERIES
HAUNTED

By Grace Cavendish

DOUBLEDAY
0 385 60853 5